To my

with

LOVE FAITH DEATH

Tara

TARA SHAH

ISBN-10:069232495X

ISBN-13:9780692324950

TO

Those humans dead or alive

whose life has been touched by

Love

Faith

Death

ACKNOWLEDGMENTS

- A big thank you to Ms. Megan Chavez Anderson of Children's House Montessori School in Lewiston, ID for help in editing, and for offering valuable feedback.
- Thanks to my husband Binay for allowing me to borrow his quotes and his personality to represent the oncologist, the simple man.
- Thanks to My sister Gamala Luitel for reading the manuscript and providing feedback.
- And most importantly, thanks to you, the reader, for reading the book.

ABOUT THE BOOK

This book is about one human's love for another regardless of their man-made identities, and socially defined relationships. This book is about faith, regardless of words used to connect to the higher being. This book is about keeping upbeat attitude and keeping hope no matter how bleak the situation might be. Learn to accept, learn to forgive, and learn to let go. After all, life in the big picture is nothing but unpredictable.

This is a story of a middle aged nurse whose life takes a different turn after she is diagnosed with cancer. Part of the story is set in Nepal (from the diary), and the other part is set in the USA. Each part from the diary starts with a date. The dates are used only to make the transition between the present and the past easy and have no other relationship to the timing of the incidences in the story.

The main character calls herself a strong feminist, and writes in her diary about the legal and social discriminations faced by women in Nepal. The definition of feminism and a feminist can be different for different people. What feminism means to Malia Obama can be different from what it means to Malala Yousafzai. To the main character of this book, feminism means being strong, being independent, and being respected as a woman. From the ability to choose a husband to obtain a passport, women in Nepal as well as many other countries are deprived of the freedom many of us in the developed world take for granted.

There are some cultural practices like palm reading and fortune telling that are mentioned in this book. These practices are common in that part of the world. People from all walks of lives including famous politicians, high rank officials, and general public rely on astrologers and fortune tellers to predict their future, advise, and guide them in their new ventures. Some of those fortune tellers are highly educated scholars in astrology but most learn the skill of fortune telling from their teachers, relatives, or another fortune teller.

In traditional Hindu marriages, it is almost impossible to make the marriage decision without first consulting an astrologer for astrological compatibility and the compatibility of cosmic influencers (commonly known as 'Grahas' in local terms) of the bride and groom to be. It is believed that the effect of those cosmic influencers (Grahas) depend on the person's time of birth. Some people born during certain time of the day/month/year are believed to have negative effects on their spouses.

The main character of the story is one of those who was born with 'Manglik' cosmic influencer, meaning that the planet Mars "Mangal Graha" was in such position in the solar system at the time of her birth that it would have strong negative effect on her husband if she married a man who was non-Manglik (a person born at the time when the planet Mars was not in such position.) What happens next changes the lives of the main characters.

As you read through the story, you may find yourself asking why she did not try to find her boyfriend early. What happened after she moved to the USA is in her purple diary that is not shared in this book. Until then, I invite you to guess and imagine what could have happened. Did she try to find him or she did not? Was he married and she did not want to be the other woman? Did she still believe in her cosmic influencers? Or had she found love again and did not think about reconnecting with him? She does not mention anything about her marriage, but does that mean that she never married anyone?

The copyrights to the songs' lyrics quoted in this book belong fully to the publishers, writers, singers or any original copyright holders of each of those songs. Neither the author nor any publisher of this book owns the copyrights to those lyrics and songs. The lyrics are used in this book only with the intention to express the mood of the characters involved and should not be considered as this book's author's words.

THE SHOCK

I did not hear anything the doctor said after I heard her say I had an "aggressive cancer." My hands were cold and shaky, my mind was fuzzy, and my jaws were trembling. I don't recall how and when I arrived home. I could not sleep in the night thinking that it could be my last night on earth. I kept telling myself it could not be true; I have taken good care of myself to minimize my risks; I can't be dying from cancer. But the biopsy results are there; telling me what I don't want to believe is the truth.

I don't recall going to the doctor for any health issues except for my annual checkups. I do not understand why cancer chose me. I can't stop asking myself - "why me?" The inner voice says everyone has to go when their purpose of being on earth is served. Do I no longer have a purpose on this earth? Or is this a punishment for something I did? What did I do wrong? I am a good human, good citizen. I helped many sick people in the hospitals; I volunteer to help the needy. I help make this world a better place for other humans. Why me?

I flipped through every cancer magazine, every cancer book, and every cancer journal I could find. I scrolled through several dozen cancer support organizations' websites, forums, and blogs to find answers. My anxiety only got worse but I did not get the answers I was looking for. I was really amazed, though, to see how much information was there. The patient support forums comforted me a little to know that I wasn't alone, but each person's journey and opinion was so different that it was almost impossible to connect the dots to apply that information to predict my outcome.

I have spent three decades of my life in the medical field. I have seen plenty of rare diseases, plenty of deaths, and plenty of sufferings. As a nurse I was trained to be empathetic, and that is what I practiced throughout my career. I often thought that I felt the patients' and the family's pain. But I never realized being in the patient's shoes was very different from being an empathetic nurse.

What does an aggressive cancer mean? Is that a nice way of saying "you are dying soon?" If so, how soon? I remember those friends, colleagues, family members and patients who survived cancer, and those who died from cancer. I can't picture myself among either of them. The desire to live has swept me far away in the memory lane as I hold onto the ropes of denial and hope. The face of my grandfather who died from cancer four decades ago keeps coming in front of my eyes.

My grandfather died in his mid-sixties, within two months of being diagnosed with cancer. At that time in Nepal, the diagnosis of cancer was equivalent of death. If one was diagnosed with cancer, one was sure to die within months if not weeks. My grandfather was sent home after he was diagnosed with cancer because there was nothing that could be done. When I first heard that he had cancer, I was extremely terrified. Everybody in the family was convinced and had accepted that my grandfather was going to die soon.

The two months that followed the diagnosis were

the most difficult time for all of us as we all helplessly watched him struggle through the pain every living moment of his life. At that time, the concept of pain management was non-existent in Nepal. The man who was the source of inspiration and courage for everyone in the family was now so miserable in pain that he begged for his death each living moment. That incident gave me nightmares for years. Decades later, I feel like I am in the same shoes, the only difference is that I have access to the world class medical services. And I know that is going to make all the difference.

THE FEAR

I was very tired when I got home from my appointment. I laid on the couch thinking about the possibility of me dying from this cancer soon. I saw an unusual envelope on the table. I had never seen anything like that before. It emitted some kind of bright light, a magnificent halo, around it. There was a thin, long piece of paper rolled inside the envelope, shining like a gold foil. As my fingers touched the envelope, my whole body felt very light as if I was floating in the air. My mind was in deep tranquility. The light from the envelope was passing through my eyes and into my mind as I read the letter.

The halo faded as soon as I finished reading the letter, and I lost that feeling of calmness and peace. Suddenly, I was filled with fear and anxiety because if what

I read in the letter were true, I will die tomorrow. But I cannot die tomorrow. I am very healthy; I always take good care of myself. I do not indulge in any unhealthy habits. I have done almost everything in the book to keep myself healthy. Could someone be playing a prank on me by sending this letter? But what about that tranquil feeling, the bright light that passed through my eyes and my mind, and that floating feeling? They were not prank, they were real.

I am too young to die. I worked my entire life hoping that I will enjoy life when I retire. Death can't be knocking at my door this soon. My daughter is getting married next year; I want to see her walk the aisle. My younger daughter is graduating from medical school, I want to see her dream of becoming a gynecologist and helping save lives of women in underserved communities come true. I want to travel the world, helping the less fortunate people. What will happen to my dreams, ambitions, plans, and wishes if I die?

I kept telling myself death cannot be so merciless. There has to be a way I can convince death to let me live; even if it is only for a little longer. I have several unfinished businesses I need to take care of before I die.

This letter must have been delivered to me by mistake. I picked up the letter again and re-read it. That was my name, and my date of birth. That was my picture in that letter. It was not a mistake. I was sweating from my head.

I thought, "maybe I can appeal it? May be I can call or email someone and request them to postpone my death." But there was no contact information in the letter. Who do I call? What do I do? There was so much I wanted to do before I died. Dying tomorrow was not one of them.

When I woke up in the middle of the night, drenched in sweat and fear, all I wanted was a warm hug. I looked at my side table several times to make sure what I just experienced was a dream, and the letter from the death wasn't there. I looked outside the window, there was a bright and happy moon smiling at me as if it knew about the dream I just had.

I closed my eyes and took a deep breathe to calm my racing heart; I felt a pair of invisible hands around my shoulder, I thanked the almighty for the warm hug. The moon said to me everything was going to be okay but I could not sleep. I decided to make the list of the things that I really wanted to do before I died.

Once I finished making the list of things I wanted to do before I died, I realized how unprepared I was to die tomorrow. I am a very organized, highly educated, and accomplished woman. Working in the medical field, I have seen death everywhere. Knowing that death is so unpredictable and can happen at any time, how ignorant and foolish I was to have lived all my life without preparing for it. I was prepared for my career, I was prepared to live against all social adversaries, I am prepared for my retirement, but I am not prepared for my death that is coming tomorrow or perhaps today?

I have had many dreams about death in the past but I never gave those dreams any more thoughts than them being just dreams. Last night's dream was different. It reminded me how much I wanted to live. It also reminded me how unpredictable life was. I don't want to die tomorrow, but I might, and I won't be able to do anything about it except being silently sucked into the dark, mysterious tunnel called death. I started visualizing my death.

My body is lying limp, lifeless, in the casket

covered with flowers. My two daughters are standing by the casket that has my lifeless body, sobbing as they hug the grieving friends and well-wishers one by one. The air in the room feels emotional; some people are talking about what a good person I was, others are busy talking about their own achievements and struggles. Some have utilized this opportunity to network with long lost contacts and even to make business deals.

As my body is being taken away to be burned to ashes, I look at the house that I called mine until I went for the last and the longest sleep of my life. The TV was still there, the couch, the dresser, the bed, the china hutch, the art collections, the latest gadgets, the diamond earrings, the closet full of designer clothes, everything was still there.

I was dead, my body was turning into ashes in a few hours and everything I had earned, I had collected, I had created, I had protected, and everything I ever called mine until now was suddenly not mine. I was leaving everything behind, including my own body.

The scariest thing about death is that it can't be seen, it can't be predicted, and you can't run away from it. I always thought I was not afraid of death, I have seen plenty of them. But the feeling I had last night when I saw the letter from death was nothing but fear. Will I be in pain? How long will I suffer? How will it affect my loved ones? Wouldn't it be beautiful if death was predictable? If each human knew when and how she or he will die?

I find myself so puny in front of death. I am not ready to die but that doesn't really matter. I want to pretend death doesn't exist. I don't want to die, ever. I don't want to think about death. But that will not make death go away. Death doesn't discriminate against anyone regardless of their race, ethnicity, gender, age, position, economic status, and anything else.

Whether you are the president, pastor, scientist, industrialist or just someone else you are guaranteed a ticket to the death's train. Last night's dream was only a reminder. Death had started to ring its bells and blow its whistles on me the moment I was conceived.

THE ACCEPTANCE

I was very angry and discouraged immediately after my diagnosis. I kept asking why me? What did I do wrong? Today I reflect back on my life and realize how privileged I have been, and what a wonderful life I have lived. I grew up in a developing country; I have seen poverty, hunger, illiteracy, diseases, and death all in one place. It was pretty common to see women carrying their newborn child in their chest and a load of firewood on their head. They used to travel for hours in the rain and in the sun to sell that firewood so that they could feed their family in the night.

When my children were small, I worried what will happen to them if I died. I wanted to be alive to see them grow, to see them lead a successful life. Now that they are grown up and successful in whatever they are doing, the desire to live has not ended. Even though I knew I had no control over death or what happens in life, I used to worry about things that were beyond my control. But over the years my perspective has changed. Nothing is bigger than its creator. And the creator has a plan for everyone.

I was not disappointed when I heard that there were no assigned guidelines, no treatment modalities for the type of cancer I had. No science is perfect for it is only knowledge, and not the phenomenon itself. Phenomena are controlled by the one who is omnipotent, omnipresent, and omniscient. Medical scientists were still trying to understand the phenomena and determine the best treatment options for this type of cancer. Doctors are just humans; they can only do what they know.

There was a small part of me that was still having a hard time accepting my diagnosis. I thought maybe the test results were wrong, or probably they got someone else's test results. I wanted to question the ability of the person who performed the tests and the person who interpreted the results. I found peace in knowing that the omnipresent, omnipotent, omniscient one that put me on this earth had a plan for me just like it has plans for every single organism on earth and beyond. There was no need to worry; everything was going to happen the way my creator intended for it to happen.

Logic says what will happen to me will totally depend on how well my treatment team seeks, interprets, and utilizes the available information, and how well my body handles what circulates through it. Since I was not ready to settle for anything less than the best, I decided to get a second opinion. I started browsing the internet in the hopes of finding a 'good doctor' that will hopefully tell me that my cancer was curable. One very familiar name caught my eyes.

My heart skipped a beat when my eyes confirmed my suspicion about the person the name belonged to. I suddenly felt a little invigorated, a little nervous, a little excited, and a little confused, all at the same time. I forgot about my diagnosis and started rowing my mind through the memory stream. The current was self-propelling but a sudden tide pushed me to the shore, and I found myself in front of the computer again. I knew that my search for a good doctor had ended here, but it gave way to another search in life that I had purposely ended decades ago.

Suddenly I realized that I did not have the time for anger, frustration, guilt, regrets, remorse, ego or any kind of negativity. There was much more to life than giving in to some mere diagnosis, and feel miserable. I opened my old suitcase and located my golden diary that used to live under my pillows once upon a time. I don't know how long I am going to live, but I have made a decision to make the remaining days of my life blissful.

THURSDAY, SEPTEMBER 6TH

I was hoping that the shifts will be a bit lighter during the holidays. But they have been busier than usual, not because we have been taking care of the sickest patients in the ICU but because we have been taking care of a so called VIP patient who is making our life miserable. He is in the ICU for no critical illness; he is the son of the home minister or some high profile politician. Of course he needed three days of ICU care for his binge drinking hangover. He really needs to be in the psychiatry ward not in the ICU.

I am not acclimated to dealing with ICU patients who can walk and talk. However, this is not the first time they have admitted someone in the ICU for some non-critical illness. Often times these so called political leaders and their pets come to the ICU to avoid jail or to seek sympathy of the general public. Visiting hours don't apply to them; they can come and go as they wish. Everybody behaves as if this patient of ours is the son- in-law of the world. In this country if you are well connected, you can be admitted to the ICU for a sore throat.

There are so many people dying every day in this same country because they don't have access to a primary care provider. Here we have these privileged people abusing the resources. Shamefully, when these not critically ill VIPs are admitted to the ICU for wrong reasons, all these so called heads of departments and the high level administrators of the hospital line up in their service. I hate to see the healthcare industry being ruled by these corrupts who exploit the system for their advantage.

Some of the people that came to visit this patient threatened to call the hospital director on me because I wasn't compassionate enough. What do they know about compassion? People who kill others for their own benefits teach me how to be compassionate. What an irony. My fault? I told them they could not come inside the ICU without wearing the ICU gown and masks. There were more than ten people in their herd; all of them wanted to come to the room together. I was just trying to keep my really critically ill patients safe by limiting the bugs these people were about to bring with them.

I hate it when they let these so called VIP people occupy the ICU bed for something that doesn't even need any medical help. That bed could have been used for someone needier. There are two other critically ill patients waiting for the ICU bed. We discharged a lady on ventilator to the medical ward to make bed available for this man. In the evening the hospital director came to visit him and ordered me to pay extra attention to his VIP guest. I wished I could say "Of course sir, we won't mind letting ten people die to save your corrupt ass friend." But I need my job so I kept quiet.

I can probably handle the constant interruptions by the visitors and phone calls by the hospital officials. But I am just so tired of the worst demeanor of this patient. He is ringing the call bell every ten minutes just to harass the staff. Besides, he has been refusing to take the medications since the day he was admitted. I honestly don't think he needs any medicine because I don't believe he is sick. I am pretty sure his hippy friends are sneaking him something else. He really needs to see a psychiatrist.

Last night he kept telling us that he wanted a doctor to give him the medications. He didn't want to deal with 'stupid nurses'. I wish I could slap his face every time he says the nurses are stupid. I am glad I was able to convince the doctor to have a psych consult for this man. In the meantime, the department head has decided that this patient will get his medications from the medical officer. I will not be surprised if they assign a doctor to deliver meals to this man.

I am an emotional person. I can't see others' pain, I can't see injustice. It frustrates me so much because I witness injustice like this and I can't do anything about it. What bothered me even more was the fact that this guy was repeatedly calling the nurses stupid and no one had the nerve to tell him that was inappropriate. If they can't respect the professionals that are vital to their health and well-being, how can they respect the rest of the people?

I feel that nurses deserve the biggest share of the credit when it comes to helping patients recover. With the exception of some 'special patients' like this gentleman who is given special attention by the doctors, we nurses are the main source of support for most of the patients and their families. It gives me an immense satisfaction when I see the critically ill patients I took care of get better and visit us in the ICU after they are discharged. That feeling of accomplishment is enough for me to keep going; I don't need these corrupt people's praise.

My job is not just a paycheck, it is someone's life in my hands, someone's trust in my judgment, and above all, it is what the god sent me to the earth for, to save lives. Does that mean I don't need money? No. I need money to do the things I want to do, and helping the less fortunate is one of them. That is why it bothers me when I have to silently watch injustice, and inhumanity take over the ones who have taken the oath to save lives.

Today I couldn't wait to come home and lie down in the bed with you, my golden diary. My mind is exhausted from all the drama of today's two shifts. Thankfully I don't have to work the morning shift tomorrow. I hope this VIP guest of ours will be discharged by the time I start my shift tomorrow. I care about my patients, and I am really proud of what I do. However, sometimes I question my love for my profession. Today I am asking myself if I became a nurse just to be harassed by the son of some corrupt minister, a corrupt hospital administrator, or a narcissist doctor.

THE HOPE

My first day at the oncologist's office was full of mixed emotions for me. I was very very scared, anxious, and sick of being sick. But I was also nervous and excited about the prospect of seeing the man I once thought I could not live without but ended up living without. I was trying to focus on my disease and all the questions I had for the oncologist, but the past that was buried in my subconscious kept distracting me. Will he recognize me? Does he even remember me? How will he react when he sees me?

It was not easy to get an appointment with this doctor. He is apparently semi-retired, and spends most of his time volunteering in different places. He only sees patients that are of his research interest. I insisted that I needed to see him no matter what. I got a call from his office stating that the doctor was interested in my case and would like to see me. I could not be any happier; I couldn't wait to see him.

The waiting area looked like an assembly of melancholists mourning the tick of the clock. Each one of them was carrying a massive but invisible timer that could stop any moment. Each of them will become limp, and lifeless the moment his/her timer stops. There was desperation in their eyes to prevent the timer from stopping. Regardless of who they were, what they did in their lives, how much wealth they had, what kind of cars they drove, what places they visited, which god they believed in, how many times they prayed, what language they spoke, what clothes they wore, they all appeared trivial in front of that massive timer they were carrying.

There were other people who also had the massive invisible timer around their neck but those people were either ignorant about the timer or were too afraid to think about it; I read no fear of the timer stopping in their eyes. They were too busy worrying about gas prices going up, their teenager behaving strangely, their neighbor parking in front of their house, their co-workers dating someone else, their bosses making their lives miserable, the wall street CEOs making millions, the other party candidate winning the election, the other religious group organizing a prayer in their neighborhoods, and so on.

Then I looked outside, the sky was covered with dark clouds, the wind was blowing with all its might, vigorously swinging the natural and man-made structures it passed through. The whistles, the roars, the cracking sounds, and the big bang, the storm was ready to swallow anything that got in its way. The rain started to run through the glass window, and the power went off. When I saw the melancholists' faces during lightning, they were still thinking about their timers, and the ignorants had more worries on their faces.

"Don't stop believing......hold on to that feeling....." "Some will win....some will lose..." The American Rock band Journey's all-time hit song kept playing in my head...

FRIDAY, SEPTEMBER 7ᵀᴴ

The alarm radio woke me up early in the morning. I forgot to turn it off last night. I wake up early on the days I don't have to go to work in the morning and can't sleep again. Why is it always like that? Since I could not go back to sleep, I decided to go jogging. It is refreshing to be out in the nature before the hustle and bustle begins. I was also longing to see the cute guy who always gives me his infectious smile and says hello when we pass by each other during our morning jogs. I didn't even know his name but I kind of felt my heart racing every time he smiled at me.

I was hoping that my VIP patient would be gone by the time I started my shift today. He was still in the ICU but he was a changed man today. The morning shift nurse told me that an intern from the psychiatry department came and talked to the patient and the patient became a different man. The patient apparently told the doctor that he never refused medication and that we never offered him any medication. He was taking all his medications without problem.

Anyway, I was happy that the beast was well tamed today. I was curious to know what the intern did to change this man's attitude but the morning shift nurse had no clue because the patient wanted to talk to the doctor only. The intern's note read, "Patient denies refusing medications. Took his 10 AM meds. Will follow up."

Tring….. tring… the telephone rang. The voice on the other end sounded somehow familiar. It was the same doctor who had convinced our VIP patient to take his medication. He asked me if the patient was taking his medications. I told him it was not time for his medication yet so I wasn't sure if he was going to take them again. The doctor asked if he needed to come during medication time. From the behavior of the patient during my shift, I was pretty confident that the patient was unlikely to refuse his medications. However, I wanted to meet the person who talked such a non-compliant person into taking his medications. So I told the intern it would be better if he was there during the medication time.

"Hello!" I heard a familiar voice coming from the door. Standing behind me was the same familiar face with the same familiar smile. It is the same guy with whom I have been exchanging hello and smile during the morning joggings.

"I didn't know you worked here." I said.

"I didn't know you worked here either." He replied. We both smiled.

"Who are you here to see?"

"I am the psychiatry department intern; I saw a patient in the morning ….."

"Oh, so you are that genius doctor who convinced him to take his medications." I interrupted him.

"Thank you for flattering me. But I am just a simple man." He humbly said.

I must say this man has something in him that makes him special. I don't know why but I felt like he did some sort of magic on me or something. I started to feel very different after talking to him; the feeling was a mix of excitement, shyness, and perhaps a little bit of romantic thoughts. I sure had a crush on him. I didn't want him to leave right after medications so I was looking for ways to keep him there. I was relieved that he also didn't show any interest in leaving. But I was a little disappointed because the whole time he was there he was talking to Rosy. They talked as if they knew each other from before. Rosy even escorted him to the break room and had coffee with him while I watched her patients.

"He seems like a nice guy." I told Rosy when she came back.

"Yeah." Rosy replied without showing much interest.

"He calls himself a simple man." I said, paying special attention to Rosy's facial expressions. I was curious to know what she thought of him.

"Oh honey, he is anything but a simple man." Rosy walked away from me.

"How do you know?" I realized my voice was a little loud.

"Why are you so interested in him?" Rosy frowned

at me.

"He is cute. I see him in the morning when I go jogging." I said.

"Are you telling me.......?" Rosy did not complete her sentence but she looked at me as if I had committed a big crime.

"No..... nothing like that. I was just curious." I felt a need to lie about my feelings to calm her down.

"He was curious about you too. He wanted to come back, I told him we had work to do. Trust me, he is going to come back tomorrow."

"Why didn't you let him come back?" I was annoyed by her indifference.

"Because I did not want him to come back. He is not right for you" Rosy gave her verdict.

Rosy is a very close friend and she does care about me like a big sister. But who is she to decide who is right for me and who is not. She literally escorted him out of the ICU. I know Rosy probably did this with my best interest in mind but sometimes I feel she is too controlling about my personal life.

SATURDAY, SEPTEMBER 8TH

I could not wait to go jogging this morning after I woke up. I woke up a little late today. I hoped that the simple man would still be there. I know his name now but I prefer to call him *'the simple man'*. He was there; waiting for me with the same contagious smile on his face.

"Hey, you are late." I noticed a different kind of friendliness in his voice today. It was not an ordinary *'hello'* anymore.

"I know." I replied sitting next to him on the bench.

"Sorry I did not get a chance to say bye to you last night." He said.

"That is okay, you can make up for that now. " I

was really in a mood to spend some time with him.

"Ok. Would you like to have some coffee?"

"Sure."

Coffee is not the most popular drink in this part of the world; partly because coffee is more expensive than tea, and partly because people prefer the taste of tea to coffee. Most people don't drink coffee at home, but some middle class people serve coffee to their special guests.

The simple man told me that he would treat me with the best coffee in town that one can only have by invitation. There are not too many coffee places in town, and I have been to almost all of them; I had never heard of such coffee place that only served coffee to invited patrons. I told him I would love to have coffee at such a special place; and of course with such a special person.

Then he led me to the interns' quarter. I didn't see this coming. He is not only nice and handsome but also has a sense of humor. The tiny kitchen in his third floor studio looked like it could really use some help. The simple man said he doesn't use the kitchen much except for making coffee for himself and his special guests. I was happy to be that special guest today. I looked around the room while the simple man washed the cups.

The apartment was as simple as it could be; nothing hanging on the wall, no TV, no curtains, no flower vases, no wall clock, no pictures. There was a small bed by the window, and a side table with alarm clock next to it. At the end of the room was a computer table and a book shelf full of books. There was a white coat and a stethoscope hanging on the side of the book shelf. I was really impressed at the simple man's modest lifestyle.

He boiled some water in the saucepan and poured the instant coffee and the milk powder into two cups while explaining to me how to make the best tasting coffee. I enjoyed watching him meticulously stir the instant coffee with a tiny spoon held between his pointer and the thumb of his right hand. The skin between his long but thin fingers was so dry that I was almost tempted to rub some moisturizer on his hands.

I am not sure if he really made the best coffee in town, like he said, or it was my mood that was making the coffee taste so good; but it was the best coffee I had ever had. And within half an hour of knowing him, I could tell that he is probably the most impressive person I have ever met. I am really amazed at how confident and logical he is. As he talks about the things he plans to do for himself and for the world, I feel positivism, optimism, and enthusiasm in his voice. From making the coffee to helping the less fortunate in the world, he seems to believe that everything under the sky is doable.

It had already been three hours, three cups of coffee, and a gazillion dollar worth conversation before I realized it was lunch time already. I completely forgot that Rosy and I had planned to take Sony for lunch today for her birthday, then go to the movies, and then do the grocery shopping. I really wanted to stay a little longer with the simple man but Rosy would have been very upset if I did so.

"Got to go." I said.

"Why? We can have lunch together." The simple man said.

"I would have loved to but I have already made plans for today." I said as I picked up my sweatshirt.

"Ok then, see you later." He smiled.

"Definitely, I will definitely see you later. I had a

great time." I opened the door.

"I enjoyed it too." The simple man walked me to the stairs.

"See you. Bye." I left.

I kept thinking about him when Rosy was making the list of things we needed for the kitchen.

"Where are you lost?" Rosy was clearly frustrated at me for not showing any interest about today's plans.

"You were with him, weren't you?" She inquired as if she was the police and I was her suspect.

While I appreciate her being such a caring friend, I don't always appreciate her trying to act like she is my mother. But I don't want to sound rude to her. She is very sensitive.

"Yes I was, he is amazing. I like him." I told her enthusiastically.

"Be careful about who you hang out with. This guy is not good for you." She warned, staring at me with her big eyes.

"Why, what's wrong with him?" I was trying to be

defiant.

"Whatever, it is your life, your choice. I am just telling you as a good friend. But why would you value my advice anymore? You have a cute handsome guy escorting you around." She can be very sarcastic at times.

Rosy stayed quiet the whole time we were out shopping, eating, and at the movies. Sony was with us so I still had fun. Sony is very fun person to be around. She asked me what happened to Rosy, but we both know Rosy goes through her upset moments every now and then so I told her it was one of those days. I am not ready to disclose my friendship with the simple man to Sony yet.

THE ALMIGHTY

I already knew my diagnosis, but I had so many questions about the disease and treatments that I did not know where to start asking. Seeing all those bald people with frail body in the waiting room scared me even more. I started thinking, "I will look like one of them pretty soon."

Most of my adult life I lived by the philosophy of not worrying about things that were beyond my control. But the diagnosis of cancer has changed me from a strong, confident, disciplined woman to a weepy, whiny, insecure melancholist. I closed my eyes and started to have a conversation with the almighty.

There was a time I searched for god in the temples,

churches, monasteries, and mosques but all I found there was ego, hatred, judgment, and lies against other humans who had a different name for their god, and a different way of connecting to their god. They all talked about heaven, and how one could find the path to heaven. Each of them emphasized that the only way to go to heaven was to follow their way of connecting to the god. I wondered if all of them were talking about the same heaven or each religion was assigned a different heaven. Are there separate heavens for Hindus, Christians, Jews, Muslims, Buddists, and those who don't assign a religion to themselves?

There was a time I pretended to be an atheist partly as a rebellion against my ultra-religious family which believed in the so called religious leaders' unconvincing rhetoric about god, and in propaganda about people of other faith, other caste, other race, and other culture to spread fear and to fuel their prejudiced mind, and partly because I was yet to find a person who could answer my questions about god.

Even as a child, I knew, if god existed, it had to be above all man made boundaries. I turned to science to prove that god did not exist only to discover that science made my faith deeper and stronger.

Being an atheist was cool; there was this notion that those who believed in science did not believe in god, only old fashioned, superstitious, ignorant people believed in god. I was told that science was making god's existence unnecessary; and I tried my best to believe in it.

The more I vested myself into the field of science, the more I realized science did not create anything, it only discovered. Science was the knowledge, and god was the phenomenon. Science could not be separated from god.

My god doesn't live in the temple or in the idols or in the heaven. I can't touch my god but I have felt my god's presence everywhere. I haven't seen my god but I talk to my god all the time. My god doesn't look like a human, nor does it look like a monkey, or an elephant.

My god doesn't have a gender, a race, a caste, a religion, a language, a nationality. My god doesn't demand that I praise it to earn its favor. My god doesn't order me to kill another person because the person calls my god by a different name, and uses different words to communicate with it.

I haven't said a formal prayer in years and I haven't been to a house of worship, a church, a temple, a mosque, or a monastery for that matter, in decades. But I am a believer. Whenever I have a question and the world doesn't have an answer, I have a problem that the world can't solve, the almighty helps me find those answers and solve those problems. My faith is the only thing that has helped me get thorough some of the toughest times in my life.

Today, once again, I am turning to my faith to help me figure this out.

TUESDAY, SEPTEMBER 19ᵀᴴ

The simple man's way of looking at the world is what I like the most about him. His optimism, his positive view of the world, and his simple but logical thinking inspire me to challenge my limits and believe in myself. Every time I meet him, I feel like I have become a wiser, happier person. I have only known him for two weeks; I already want to spend my whole life with him. Oh god I can't believe I am so much in love with the simple man.

I couldn't stop thinking about the simple man at work last night. This guy is so addictive. I briefly saw him yesterday in the cafeteria; it was not a planned meeting but we spent half an hour talking. I wanted to see him again. I wondered how he felt about me. It is also possible that he has many other girls like me who are invited for his special coffees. I also wondered why Rosy kept saying that he is not good for me? Does she know anything about him that I should be aware of? But why would she not tell that to me if it was something really bad?

He is very assertive, and I have noticed that some people find his high level of self-confidence a little threatening. They call him arrogant. If you are humble, people think you are timid, if you are assertive, people think you are arrogant. That is why I say what others think of me is not my business. But Rosy is not just another person, she is a very close friend and she would not do anything to harm me. That is why I need to know why Rosy thinks he is not good for me.

"Hello!" There he was at the door, smiling. He showed up in the ICU. My heart was ready to skip a beat. Then he went to the other nurse and started asking her about the patient with suicidal attempt that he had seen in the morning.

"He did not come to see me…." I thought to myself. I felt betrayed; perhaps by myself, by my feelings. I tried to keep myself busy at the bedside as he engaged in conversation with another nurse at the nursing station. But

I couldn't concentrate. I needed a break.

He came to me and said in a loving voice, "hey, you seem pretty busy."

My heart skipped a beat again. Why do I feel this way whenever I hear his voice or I see his face?

"No, not really….." I replied to him and went to the nursing station. I was pretending to keep distance with him.

"Jasmine, would you mind if I take a break now?" I asked the other nurse.

"Go ahead hun." Jasmine enthusiastically replied.

"It was nice to see you." he waved his hands at the other nurse and followed me as I walked out the door.

"Hey doc, you stay here for a little bit more." Jasmine yelled. Rosy hates it when these middle aged married women try to flirt with all these young doctors. I didn't really care before but today I am also uncomfortable that Jasmine is trying to flirt with the simple man.

"I am not working tonight, I just came to see my friend." He replied to Jasmine.

"So you are not here to see the OP poisoning patient?" I somehow felt the need to hear from him that he was really here to see me.

"Nope. I came to see you." His answer was very straight forward.

"How nice of you. But I am working." I was elated to hear that but I pretended that I was more interested in my work than in him.

"I know madam. I won't hurt your work. Patients come first." I wished I could hold his hands and talk with him all night but the simple man says patients come first.

"So.....?" I asked him.

"So can we have coffee together when you are taking your break?" He always has a plan.

"I will die to have a coffee with you my simple man....screw work...........not really....may be....I don't know.... ...oh......" I thought to myself.

My heart was pounding. My cheeks were blushing. But I was afraid that the other nurses will start spreading rumor if I spent time alone with him while I was working. I know these women specialize in defaming others.

"You know Jasmine? She is going to make a big deal about it." I reluctantly told him.

"About what?" He looked surprised.

"About you visiting me at work." I told him.

"Is it illegal to meet with someone when they are on break?

"No, but you have no idea what she is capable of doing. She will spread all kind of rumors."

"What others think doesn't really bother me. I don't waste my time and energy in worrying about what others will think." He said in his firm voice.

"That is true. It doesn't bother me either." I said to him but it was bothering me already. He is a man, rumors do not affect men. But I am a girl, it affects me. I like to spend time with the simple man, but I don't like people to be talking about my relationship with him.

Jasmine made several trips to the break room during those thirty minutes that I was there with the simple man. She ordered me in after thirty minutes because she needed to make an urgent phone call. There was no reason for her to call me in that quickly.

50

THE STORM

Is it a co-incidence? Or was it meant to happen? Why did time throw me into this situation after all these years? It will be inappropriate to say that I had forgotten him because there was not one day in last thirty years that I did not think of him but I had learned to live without him. In fact, I lived a very successful life without him. I was strong, I was in control, I was happy. Ever since I saw the simple man's name, I feel vulnerable again. I am losing control, and I am stressed. I know I had an option to go to another doctor but I chose not to because I could not control myself. How can I pass an opportunity to meet my simple man, the love of my life?

"The wait is really long today." I told the

receptionist. "The doc is not here yet, your appointment is at one I believe." The receptionist replied in a kind voice. I looked at my watch, I had hardly been there for an hour and it was not even time for my appointment yet. But it felt like I had been there my entire life. I left home early because I did not want to get caught in that storm. I had thought that many people would not show up because of the weather and I might get to see the doctor earlier than my appointment but the waiting room was full of patients.

There were people of all ages in the waiting area. A beautiful girl in her late teens, a mother of a toddler, an eighty-nine year-old lady, a war veteran, a teacher, an artist, a nurse, and so on; cancer did not spare any of us. It did not consider the girl was too young, the woman had young children, the lady's body was too old and frail to fight it, the artist had a big show coming soon, and I had a bucketful of things to do before I died.

I guess the storm outside does not bother you when you are dealing with a hurricane that is wiping out everything inside you. There was an elderly man pacing in the hallways, sweating from his forehead. The woman accompanying him was repeatedly asking him to sit down but he was too restless to sit. I asked him if he was in pain and if he needed immediate attention. The man looked even more annoyed and replied in an agitated voice, "You can't help me. I am dying." I wasn't quite sure what was wrong with him but I apologized to him, and asked the receptionist if he could be seen as soon as possible.

Twenty minutes later the man came out of the exam room with a big smile on his face. Before I could say anything, he apologized to me and said that he wasn't dying anymore. He went on telling me the reason for his restlessness earlier. He was referred to the cancer doctor and that made him think that he might have cancer. But his disease turned out to be a non-malignant blood disorder. The cancer doctor was also a blood doctor. Since the name of the clinic suggested that the clinic was a cancer center, the couple had reasons to be anxious.

Then he told me that today he drove his antique car that he had treasured in his garage for many decades. He did so because he thought he had cancer and he might die soon. "I thought I might as well enjoy this beauty before I die. Now she will go right back to her place." He was concerned that the storm might have caused some damage to his beauty but he said the good news was worth it. His wife joked about how he used to spend more time with his beauty than with his wife when they were newly married.

The young lady in the chair next to me asked me if I was there to see the simple man as well. When I told her it was my first visit, she started telling me how much she liked her oncologist. She was his long term patient and had been cancer free for some time. "I am here today just to thank him. He saved my life." The lady looked so good that I initially thought she must be a family member or a friend of one of the patients. It is always encouraging to see so many people getting cured of their cancer.

Louis Armstrong's "and I think to myself.....what a wonderful world......" was playing in my mind.

TUESDAY, DECEMBER 21ST

Rosy is creating a big drama about my relationship with the simple man. For some ridiculous reason, she thinks I should not be close to the simple man. We had an argument about it last week and she stopped talking to me after that. Rosy insisted that it was her responsibility to stop me from making bad choices. She thinks she is only trying to do what a good friend is supposed to do. But what I can't make her understand is that I am an adult and I have a fair understanding of what is good or bad for me. She got really mad when I told her I did not need her approval when deciding who I can hang out with.

Rosy has been staying in her apartment and crying all the time. She has not gone to work since Friday. She says she wants to die. I don't know what to do; I don't know if she is really depressed or if she is just being manipulative. This whole thing started since we had a fight last week over my relationship with the simple man. I told Sony about it; she came over to visit Rosy this morning but Rosy did not talk to Sony either. The root of Rosy's distress is my relationship with the simple man, and that makes me angry.

I love Rosy, she is my best friend. There are no secrets between us. But I do not understand why sometimes the people who love you the most are the ones who turn out to be against your happiness. I thought I knew Rosy so well, but she has been a stranger lately.

I met Rosy in college. We became best friends only in the final year of college while studying for the exams. Rosy used to come to my hostel room, which I shared with three other friends, to study for the exams; we used to fall asleep in my bed while studying. The beds in our hostel were pretty small to fit two people but having another human next to you was the best way to keep warm at night during the cold winters. I did not mind sharing the bed with Rosy. Exams were over but Rosy never slept in her own bed again.

After college, Rosy became even more important part of my life. She is not only close to me but also close to my family and close relatives. She treats them like her own family and they treat her like theirs too. I have also met most of her family. We go to each other's houses during holidays and festivals. We work in the same place. We have separate apartments but Rosy's apartment is used mostly for guests only.

Rosy likes to make lunch for me and even brings it to work on days I am working and she is not. Until few days ago, we used to sleep in the same bed, eat in the same kitchen, and spend most of our time together. The only time we were apart was when we were working different shifts. But she moved back to her apartment last week after we had the fight about the simple man. Rosy had made dinner that night but I had already made plans to have dinner with the simple man. I invited her to join us for dinner but she refused.

Today Rosy told me that she doesn't want to lose me. From the very beginning, Rosy has been kind of possessive about me. She wants to influence even the smallest things in my life, including who I become friendly with. I have noticed that Rosy gets jealous if I hang out too much with other girls. But I did not think that she would feel the same way if I started hanging out with a man. I don't know how I can help her grow up. I think it is about time that Rosy finds a boyfriend for herself.

I do not understand why Rosy is not able to differentiate the relationship between me and the simple man from the relationship between me and her. I am pretty sure she doesn't expect me to live my whole life with her. We both plan to get married one day. We have talked at least thousand times about how our future husbands will look like, talk like, behave like etc. I have seen excitement in her eyes every time she talks about her dream husband. I know she hopes to find a man who will treat her like a queen. Then why does she think my relationship with the simple man will damage my relationship with her?

In our society the parents or guardians decide who their children will marry. But that doesn't stop us from dreaming about our life partners. Rosy and I have very different choices when it comes to life partners. Rosy says the man who will marry her needs to be handsome, needs to make good money, and needs to worship her. I want an honest, confident, responsible, and intelligent man who will inspire and encourage me every single day. I want a man who will not only love me for my strengths but also challenge me to face my fears, my weaknesses, and my negative thoughts so that I can be a better person.

Rosy can find a good person to marry her any time she wishes. She is beautiful, she is educated, she has good job, and her family is wealthy and influential socially. Many people have brought several proposals but Rosy has been turning her deaf ear on all of them. People come to me first when they bring marriage proposal for Rosy. They think I can influence her marriage decision but that is not true. I have asked her to take those marriage proposals seriously but she never did. She made sure to collect all of their pictures though.

SUNDAY, JANUARY 7TH

Rosy threw about half a dozen pictures at me and Sony today and told us to pick a guy for her. She had finally made up her mind about marriage after two weeks in hibernation. From outside, Rosy likes to exert control and sometimes even act bossy but deep down she feels insecure and is afraid to make decisions for herself. She said she will marry any guy we picked for her because she was ready to experiment her life. I love her, I want her to be happy, but I can't make decisions for her.

How can anyone make a decision about who to marry by just looking at their pictures? People say marriages are made in heaven, and there is someone for everyone. If heaven exists and if marriages are really made in heaven, it wouldn't matter who we picked from the picture. But we can't give up on perfection. We started analyzing each picture closely for all clues we had learned in the psychology classes about posture, body language, body structure, facial features etc. On the back of each picture was the guy's name, zodiac sign, occupation and contact person's name

I had looked at those pictures for so long that all of those faces are coming in front of my eyes right now. A few of them were really cute guys. If husbands were only for decoration, I will definitely marry those cute guys in a heartbeat, perhaps all of them. But we have higher expectations from our spouses, and the cute face doesn't tell if they will keep up with the expectations. After scanning the pictures and discussing them extensively, we decided that Rosy will meet with all of them before making her decision.

Rosy is not the only one being pressured to get married. I also get plenty of those proposals. I have told my parents that I will not get married until I complete my bachelors degree. My parents have been supportive of that idea but they still get tempted by constant pressures from friends and relatives. The other day, mom called me about another proposal that came from a close relative's friend. Mom told me to seriously think about it despite me reminding her that I still had more than a year before I would complete my bachelors degree.

The simple man has everything I want in a life partner. He is honest, logical, persistent, courageous, and extremely positive. He challenges me to think differently and to look for the positive side in everything. The simple man has taught me that I need not impress anyone but myself. I feel stronger, happier, and wiser when I am with him. I want to feel that way for the rest of my life. But the simple man plans to go to America, and I don't know what his thoughts are about marriage. I don't feel comfortable asking.

THURSDAY, FEBRUARY 23ᴿᴰ

Today Rosy is meeting with one of those candidates who could possibly be her husband. She decided to meet this guy first because he looked really handsome in the picture, and he lived abroad, two of the many criteria Rosy has for her future husband. If both Rosy and the handsome guy liked each other, they will get married, perhaps next month. She has asked me to go with her tonight to meet this guy. Even if it doesn't work out, according to Rosy, it is fun to spend an evening with a handsome guy.

Before I met the simple man, I used to think that I will also marry a stranger my parents or some concerned relatives chose for me, just like my friends, cousins, sisters, aunts, and pretty much every other girl I know did, and have been doing for centuries. But the idea of marrying someone unknown does not appeal to me anymore. I can't imagine marrying someone I don't love, or I have met only for the purpose of marrying. But Rosy is different. She is not against marrying a stranger.

Rosy's brothers have been pushing her for marriage ever since she graduated from high school. Her father went against her brothers' wish and let her go to college and work as a nurse. Rosy believes her father favors her over her brothers because she takes care of her family better than her brothers do. According to Rosy, her brothers just want her father's money. Now her father is getting older and is ailing, he wants to see her married before his death.

Rosy's family dynamics are very different from that of mine. Her father is a wealthy man who owns lots of lands and properties valued at very high prices. He has three wives, the first he married when he was twelve years old, and then he married his second wife after few years because the first wife could not give him any children. Both of these marriages were arranged by his parents. Later in his forties, he met Rosy's mother, a woman twenty-five years younger, during his business trips to the city. Rosy's mother was his housekeeper in the city; they both fell in love and secretly got married.

Rosy's parents could not keep their marriage a secret for too long because Rosy was growing in her mother's womb. Rosy's grandfather was very authoritative and powerful in the family. No one could go against his will. Rosy's father already had two wives and three sons, therefore, he was afraid that his father would not approve of his relationship with Rosy's mother. However, Rosy's grandfather, who himself was a husband to four wives, accepted the third daughter-in- law without hesitation. Rosy's mother quickly won her father-in-law's heart.

Rosy's step brothers were already teen-agers when Rosy was born. They were not happy about the fact that their father gave more attention to Rosy and her mother than his sons and their mothers. Rosy was different than all of her brothers. Unlike her brothers, she always excelled in her studies and was very caring to her family.

Despite their father's effort to send them to private schools and hire private tutors, her brothers never finished college. Since they did not do well in the study, their father got all of them married and gave them their share of his wealth.

The laws of this country are very discriminative against women. Daughters do not have any rights to their father's wealth unless they stay unmarried until the age of 35. Rosy cannot legally inherit her father's wealth if she gets married now. And she will have to return the assets if she gets hers father's assets after 35, and then gets married. But her father can give some assets to her as a dowry, in which case, the assets will be actually given to her husband or his family, and not to her.

Even though only sons are legally entitled to their father's wealth, Rosy's father divided part of his assets among his sons and his wives, and kept the highest share for himself. He told his family that he will transfer his share of the wealth to that person who takes care of him at his old age. Rosy's brothers wanted Rosy to get married as soon as possible because they were afraid that their father will give his assets to Rosy.

SATURDAY, FEBRUARY 25TH

We arrived a few minutes early at the restaurant where Rosy was meeting the handsome guy. The restaurant looked dark, almost scary, from outside when we approached the entrance. I looked at Rosy, she was blushing and almost shaky. I held her hands, they were cold like ice. I asked her "Are you ok?" She nodded. I reminded her to take a deep breath as we entered the room.

The lights automatically turned on as we approached the door. Rosy looked stunning in that purple dress that was loosely flowing from her waist. Her dark big eyes shone in the light just like bright stars shining in the sky. A guy in white shirt signaled us to the table at the end of the hall. I heard some noise behind the wall, but the hall we were directed to was empty. The candles inside the orange oval bulbs on the tables were making a pleasant scent; the chairs were organized in the shape of a heart.

"This is romantic...." I whispered in Rosy's ears. She pinched me on my thigh before I could say anything else. A tall, handsome man in black suit and a lean man with French cut beard were coming towards us. The lean man introduced himself to us as the handsome man's best friend. The handsome guy needed no introduction as we had seen his picture for long enough to remember his face for rest of our lives.

The French bearded man signaled the handsome man and Rosy to the door that led to the garden. Once Rosy and the handsome man were out the door, the lean man pulled one of the chairs that made the shape of the heart, and signaled me to sit on it.

"This is really nice.....kind of romantic..... I didn't even know this place existed." I smiled at him and walked away. The wall on my left had a beautiful mural of ancient Indian village *Dwaraka*.

"This is a lucky place. Whoever meets a girl here ends up marrying her." The French bearded man whispered in my ears almost resting his chin over my shoulder.

I wasn't comfortable with his overly friendly mannerism but I was the girl's best friend and he was the guy's best friend. I thought perhaps he was just trying to be nice to me.

"Really? That's interesting!" I replied without looking at him.

"If a man pulls a chair forming this heart and the girl sits on the chair, it is believed that the girl will be trapped in his heart forever." The French bearded man explained enthusiastically.

I just smiled and continued looking at the murals on the wall.

"I have heard a lot about you." He said.

"About me? How come?" I smiled again, pretending to be friendly.

He told me that he does a thorough research on a girl before he approves any girl for his friends or cousins.

And he expressed frustration over how hard it is to find a good, pure, and cultured bride these days. He was also disappointed about many educated girls having boyfriends. Then he started bragging about himself, his job, how many girls he has rejected, how connected he is politically, and what he thinks about gender equality and feminism.

During the conversation, I also learned that there were some other members of the handsome man's family parked at all corners of the restaurant to evaluate Rosy without her knowledge. He also mentioned that many of the handsome's family members had already seen Rosy and perhaps interacted with her but Rosy may not have been aware of that. The French bearded man was emphasizing on how extensive their selection process was, and how lucky Rosy was to be the one to meet his best friend.

"So Rosy passed your exam?" I was pretending to engage in the conversation. It had been more than half an hour since they went to the garden but there was no sign of Rosy and the handsome man coming inside.

"Yes. So did you; in fact with flying colors." He gave me his half foot smile.

"Me? So you did a research on me too?" My voice

was a little loud and my heart was pounding.

Thanks to my intuitive instincts, I could sense what he was thinking. I was starting to get annoyed but reminded myself to keep my cool.

"Yes. It was my personal interest," he winked at me and smiled again, "you know sometimes you have to think about yourself too."

"But I am not the one getting married." I replied without turning my eyes away from the murals.

"Of course you will get married if you find the right guy, won't you?"

I startled as he approached me from the back; he had two cups of coffee in his hands, he extended one to me.

"I don't drink coffee at night." I told him as I moved away from him trying to find my personal space.

"How much longer do you think they will take?" I wanted him to know that I had no interest in conversing with him anymore.

"Don't worry about them," he continued after he

put the coffee on the table and moved to the chair next to me, "I want to talk about us."

I have a strong aversion against these kinds of traps. I am a serious person, and I don't flirt with anybody. I felt almost like I was being taken lightly. And, I dislike men who take me lightly. I hate to be in a situation for which I am not prepared. I was visibly agitated at this point but Mr. French beard did not seem to give up. I managed to control myself and gave the conversation a 180 degree turn.

"I love this art; do you know who painted these murals?" I asked him even though I had already seen the artists' names on the wall.

"I didn't know you are into arts and paintings." He looked surprised.

"I am just an admirer. My boyfriend loves to paint." I was looking for an opportunity to bring up 'my boyfriend' in the conversation so he would stop attempting to flirt with me.

"Your brother loves to paint?" He pretended to have misheard what I said.

"I said my boyfriend loves to paint, not my brother. I don't have a brother." I said, looking right into his eyes, my heart was dancing with victory.

"I didn't know that." He said in a soft, weak tone. I saw the color on his face changing from yellow to red to dark red. His ears were so red as if they were going to bleed. Clearly, this is not something he expected to hear.

The simple man is a pure science person who knows nothing about arts, not excluding music. In fact, he is the first and perhaps only person I have met who doesn't know full lyrics of even one song.

It looked like the lie about my boyfriend worked pretty well; the French bearded man did not talk much after that. I felt as if I had hit the biggest jackpot of all time.

THE PARADISE

The walls of the waiting area at the doctor's office were full of posters with information about cancers, and the services offered by the facility. My brain was already overloaded with all the information from internet and medical journals; I had no desire to read any of that information on the walls. But my eyes were caught by one poster that had information on my cancer. This was one of the very few studies conducted on the type of cancer I had. The study was recently presented at a national meeting of the cancer doctors and was yet to come in print. As I suspected, the investigator was no one but the simple man.

The nurse called me into the examination room. I

had already filled out twenty pages of paper works, and the nurse was about to give me more to complete. I have been in their shoes and I know why they require so much of documentation, but for cancer patients like me who already has so much to worry about and to endure, the extra paperwork are an added nuisance. The nurse promised I would not be required to fill out those many papers during subsequent visits.

It is very frustrating for the healthcare providers too; I used to find myself often caught between my personal ethics and professional duty when I had to make decision about whether to spend the time actually providing care to my patients or repeatedly copying/pasting the same information in several pages of medical records. The rules are there for a reason, so rather than wasting my energy in complaining about them, I quickly signed all the papers she handed me returned them to her.

"The doc will be in soon." The nurse told me before she headed to the door. In anticipation of meeting my simple man after all these years, I was feeling very nervous. I almost wanted to ask the nurse to stay with me when the doctor was in the room. But if she asked me why, I didn't know what to say. I knew she had lots of work to do; I thought it would be better to let her finish her work than have her stay with me.

My hands and feet were sweating, I was breathing heavily.

"Are you alright?" The nurse asked me.

"I am fine, just a little nervous." I told her.

"If you would like, I can stay with you until the doc comes in. You can talk to me if there is anything that is bothering you." The nurse was very compassionate.

"No, I will be fine." Part of me wanted the nurse to be with me when the simple man was in the room but the other part wanted some privacy, just me and the simple man.

The nurse left.

"Surreal." I told to myself when I looked outside the window. The paradise was in front of my eyes.

WEDNESDAY, FEBRUARY 29TH

Rosy had already spent an hour with the handsome guy. I was so annoyed by the French bearded man that I was thinking about telling Rosy to reject the handsome man. But it will be unfair to Rosy if I judged the handsome man by his friend. Rosy looked happy on her way back home. I was curious to know what she thought of him.

"So you liked him?" I asked her.

"You know, he is handsome; and pretty smart too. What do you think?" She sounded really excited.

"Well, I don't know. I didn't like his friend for sure. He was seriously trying his luck with me. He even said he did a thorough research on me and you...." I told Rosy about everything that happened.

"Are you serious? That is disgusting." Rosy was really offended to know that the handsome man came with half a dozen family members to evaluate her, and he didn't even tell her about that.

Something that bugged us both was that he wasn't honest. If he was, he would have told her about his family that was inside the restaurant watching every move Rosy made. He also sounded like he either lacked self-confidence or valued others' opinion too much to the point that he felt the need to bring half a dozen family members to evaluate Rosy for him.

The other thing that upsets both of us the most is that the handsome man's brother has two wives. The brother married second wife because his first wife became paraplegic during a motor vehicle accident. The brother has three young daughters with his first wife. Both Rosy and I are strong feminists; we don't like people who are not respectful to women. We are advocates of fairness and justice. To us, it is not fair to the brother's first wife that her husband married someone else after she became disabled.

Rosy said the handsome guy tried to justify the second marriage of his brother, citing the circumstances at home and social issues. Rosy and I have seen plenty of injustice and unfair treatment of women in the society. Polygamy is pretty rampant in the society. Both my maternal grandfather and paternal grandfather have two wives. One of my maternal uncles also has two wives. Rosy's father has three wives. But Rosy is not prepared to marry a man who supports polygamy. So the decision was made, the handsome guy was rejected. That night we talked about how scared we both were about marrying someone unknown.

Rosy's step brother called me at work the morning after he found out that Rosy had decided against marrying the handsome guy. He accused me of brainwashing Rosy and talking her out of marrying such a perfect person.

According to him, "daughters are someone else's treasures. The job of the family is to raise her into a cultured, respectful, caring woman so that she can take care of her husband's family. The reason her parents educate her is not to enable her to disobey her parents and defame her family but to help her be successful in her life as a married woman - a wife, a daughter- in -law, and a mother."

I also got calls from another person who had initially brought the proposal. She asked me to convince Rosy to marry the handsome guy because, according to her, Rosy will never find such a "jewel". She said, "any girl will be lucky to be married to him."

Rosy is very vulnerable at this moment. She will probably marry the handsome guy if I encouraged her to do so, but I can't force her to go against what she stands for. The decision to reject the handsome guy was Rosy's, not mine. I did what a good friend would do, I supported her decision.

In a society where our parents' generation met their spouses for the first time at the wedding stage, it is almost impossible to make anyone understand that I am not comfortable about making a decision about whether or not to marry someone after meeting the person for one hour.

Child marriage was a way of life until couple of decades ago. Almost all women from my grandmother's generation got married before they started their first menstrual cycle, most of them being married between five to seven years of age. Women from my mother's generation got to be as old as fifteen to eighteen years before they were too old to get married.

I grew up seeing many women who were widowed at the age of seven or eight and never remarried. They spent all of their lives working like a servant for their brothers or other relatives. Those who remarried or had physical relationship with other men were condemned by the society. They were not eligible to take part in any sacred rituals. Children born out of such relationships were also given lower status in the society. These rules did not apply to men. Men had and continue to have no restriction on how many times they get married and at what age.

The society is rapidly changing but so many things still remain the same as they were before. The age at which girls get married has changed now, and girls go to schools and are obtaining higher education but they are still discouraged from selecting their own husbands. Widows are still discouraged from remarrying. A widow is expected to mourn her dead husband for her whole life by not wearing colorful clothes and not grooming. Widows are treated as a sign of misfortune and are often discouraged from participating in auspicious occasions. On the other hand, men start looking for a new wife the moment they return from their wife's funeral.

Rosy was firm in her decision about the handsome man. This was one of those rare situations when a woman had rejected the man, and not the other way around. It is pretty common for a man and his family to reject a girl after meeting with her, but it is almost unlikely for a girl or her family to reject a man after the meeting. Besides, the handsome guy was not just about anyone. He was handsome, he lived in the UK, and he was from a well-connected family. He could be one of the most sought after bachelors even among educated girls' circle.

The handsome guy and his family found it very insulting that Rosy had rejected him. They tried questioning Rosy's (and mine) character in an attempt to defend their ego.

FRIDAY, APRIL 17TH

The handsome guy married one of the girls who worked in our hospital. We heard that the girl needed to be rushed to the emergency room with third degree tear on the first night after their wedding. The cause of the tear was obvious, everybody made fun of the situation, some thought he was just "real big" there.

Nobody seemed to care there could be more to the situation than what we enjoy talking about. I am no sex expert but I have never heard of someone having a third degree tear during a consensual intercourse. In this society, husbands have a license to rape their wives, who am I to question?

I am pretty sure this is not an isolated incident but

we very seldom hear about these issues. Women's private parts are so stigmatized that even if she had to endure forceful, non-consented sexual attack from her husband, and even if she suffered tear or other injuries to her genitalia, no newlywed bride will have courage to talk about the trauma with anyone, let alone seek help. This girl was brave enough to go to the emergency room for the tear. I am thankful that Rosy did not marry that man.

These kinds of incidents remind me how special the simple man is. He and I have spent hours together inside closed rooms talking about both silly and serious things but he never tried to take advantage of the situation. We are very close to each other, he tells me all those dirty jokes, he is helping me get out of my comfort zone in discussions about physical intimacy, but he knows I am not ready to take the plunge and he has never insisted me to do so.

I love him, I am also curious about how that special intimacy will feel like, and I would like to experience that with him than with anyone else. And I am sure the simple man is also eager for the same. We both know sooner or later it will happen, there is nothing to rush, nothing to push each other for. When the right time comes, it will happen itself, and it will be blissful, it will be special, no regrets, no force, just love.

Rosy and I both have realistic expectations about what we want in our husbands. We want a man who respects women; we want a friend who is honest, supportive, and understanding. We have decided to take our chance and refuse to settle for anything less.

Keeping her fantasy about finding a picture perfect husband aside, Rosy has made a decision to meet a guy who is not so good looking, is about the same height as her, does not live in foreign country, and has no socio-political connections. He is average at best. We will know more about him after meeting him tomorrow.

THE FLASHBACK

My heart skipped a beat when I heard the knock on the door. I woke up to the reality, I am a cancer patient in the doctor's office, and the man in front of me is the doctor who I have chosen to be my partner in this fight. This is the same man I had once hoped will be my partner in life and in death, in health and in sickness, in heaven and in hell.

But the life's boat sailed on a different direction; and eventually, thirty years later, brought me in front of him, proving once again that the world is round. No matter which direction you sail, you will reach your destination because there is apparently only one destination for all of us; the paths we choose could be different.

"Surreal, isn't it?" he said with a smile as he approached the sink to wash his hands.

"Surreal. Yes. That is exactly what I was thinking."

We used to do this mind reading game back in the days. Often times he would say the exact same thing I had in my mind.

He used to say he was telepathic and I used to say, "this is mind syncing because we are made for each other." He used to laugh when I said that.

He never agreed or disagreed about my 'made for each other' remarks. He later revealed that his telepathy worked on me only.

"So, your telepathy still works." I almost wanted to say but I controlled myself.

He had a medical student with him; I did not want to make him uncomfortable in front of the medical student. Besides, I was not sure if he still remembered me, and even if he did we were in very different situation. That was our past and this is our present. At this time, I am a cancer patient and he is my doctor. The only thing that was important in that room was my health. I tried hard to switch my mind gear back to present from the past but that familiar face kept distracting me.

Once I found the simple man and made him in-charge of my health, I did not feel the need to research about my disease. The simple man I once knew was the best, and I am confident that he is still the best.

I spent the last few days before my appointment researching about him. Even though I met him after thirty years, my heart knew he was the same simple man it never stopped loving. Everything that was buried in my sub-conscious started coming in front of my eyes.

"My world is empty without you..." the popular song by the Supremes keeps playing in my head.........

Rosy and I went to meet with the average guy last week. Unlike the handsome guy who we met at a fancy restaurant, we met the average guy at a mutual friend's house. It was a very casual and comfortable environment. Rosy and the average guy went outside to the patio while I chatted with the friend and his wife. Within minutes of meeting her, I realized that the friend's wife and I had so much in common.

We love art, literature, culture, and history, we both are interested in philanthropic causes, we both are active feminists, and we both love cooking. We are so much alike that by the time I left her house, I felt like I had known her forever. Like me, she is trying hard to lose those extra pounds from around her waist. She was complaining about not being able to lose her weight despite eating very little. I borrowed the simple man's words to give her some insights on the physiology of weight gain and loss.

Human body is like a bank account, the simple man says. If you keep depositing money into your bank account and don't spend or spend less than what you deposit, then your bank account will keep fattening. Similarly, if you keep depositing more energy in your body than you can expend, the unconsumed energy will result in the horizontal growth of your body. In other words, if you eat more calories than your body can burn, the extra calories will deposit in the form of fat and you will gain weight.

We both acknowledged that one important but often forgotten aspect of weight loss strategies is to keep a food journal. While keeping a food journal sounds like such a simple task, I can tell from my own experience that it requires a great deal of efforts. One needs to be disciplined and dedicated to make any kind of change in one's life; whether it is losing weight, quitting cigarettes, getting a college degree, or managing money, success comes with self-discipline.

The simple man believes adults are less disciplined than children because self-disciplining requires conscious efforts most of us aren't willing to put. He says if you don't discipline yourself, someone else will discipline you. I agree with him, it is easier to slack when you are in-charge of yourself.

I struggle with self-disciplining issues all the time. Like any other ambitious person, I want to be successful in personal and professional life. The parameters used to measure success can be different for everyone, and they change as the person's situation changes. To me success is to make my life meaningful, for myself not for someone else. Therefore, while I keep my eyes constantly on my target, I live my life one day at a time. Nobody knows who will be here tomorrow and who won't.

The transient nature of life is what motivates me to get the most out of my day; I practice self-discipline so that I can close my eyes at night and feel peace as I go to sleep knowing that I will have no regrets even if I don't wake up tomorrow because I have lived a fulfilling life. It amazes me how much, as a society, we emphasize on being happy. But in my personal experience, happiness comes with success, and success comes with self-discipline, which most of us lack.

When I got my first job as a registered nurse, I suddenly found myself as an independent twenty -year-old who had more money than she could manage, more free time than she ever had, and no one to discipline her. I was no longer the teenager living in a hostel with a small allowance from her parents every month, and whose only job was to study. The new job not only gave me the money and independence but also opened a whole new world for me. It was very easy to feel lost in that new world.

Before I met the simple man, there was a constant battle in my mind between the perfectionist me and the slacker me. The slacker me tried to convince the perfectionist me that I had worked hard all these years, and now was the time to enjoy life. I was surrounded by people just like me, young, fun loving girls with no life experience. Spending time in things that were unproductive and spending money in things that were not necessary became my lifestyle. But deep down I was not happy. The perfectionist me asked the slacker me if I wanted to live my life like this, and the answer was loud and clear - NO. I needed to change myself.

When I made the decision to change, I did not think it would be that hard. I not only had to resist the temptation to do all the fun things that I loved doing with my friends, I also had to gather a great deal of courage to repeatedly say no to my friends' invitation to those parties, movies and shopping trips, and risk offending them.

I still wanted to hang out with my friends, I still wanted to be liked by them, and I still wanted them to believe that I was the same person they once knew. But it is hard to be different while pretending to be the same. It wasn't too long before I was an outcast.

I realized that it didn't matter if my friends approved my decision to change or not, because they will not be there to share the consequences of the choices I made in my life. Every time I lost motivation, I asked myself whether I could close my eyes peacefully if I were to die right that moment. I could not quit trying until I could convince myself that I had given my best. Just like the simple man says, the results are not in your hands but the efforts are. The hardest thing to change was not my routine but my perception of myself.

I had to overcome the fear of being judged; take

the risk of being labeled 'weirdo' because I had chosen to live differently. At that moment I realized how much I valued someone else's opinion of me over my own. Consciously and unconsciously, I constantly seek others' approval of me. What I did, how I lived, how I talked, how I thought, everything was shaped by my perception of what others thought of me. I hated to be judged but, ironically, I found myself seeking judgments all the time.

Then the simple man came into my life. His positivism and determination radiated to me, and strengthened my will power to overcome the odds. He helped me realize that when I decided to break away from the habits and the people I thought were not good for me, I was making judgments about them.

I no longer cared what others thought of me because judging others and being judged was part of everyone's life. The judgments affect you only to the extent you allow them to affect yourself.

Rather than wasting my energy on building relationships that broke me down, I focused on strengthening those that built me up. The results of positive change affect not only the person who takes the leap but also those around her. Like anything new, at first there was resistance, then denial, and then finally acceptance of the new me, from myself and from my friends. Rosy was the first one to be affected by my change, and soon I found myself with a team again.

When I told my secrets to the friend's wife, she was totally amazed. I couldn't believe I had just opened my heart to a stranger without worrying about being judged.

Besides Rosy, I haven't talked about the simple man with anyone else. Not that it is a secret, many people who work in the hospital have seen us together, and probably know about us, but I had never talked to anyone so openly about me and the simple man. When Rosy came inside after two hours, I saw the contentment on her face. I knew it was an evening well spent with strangers.

MONDAY, JUNE 15TH

There was no need to ask Rosy what she thought of the average guy because it was all over her face. I was still curious to hear more about her interaction with him. We could not talk about it that night because I was working the night shift, and went to work directly from the friends' house. The average guy and the friend dropped Rosy off at her apartment. The next morning when I came back from work, Rosy was working the morning shift. I had the rest of the week off so I went to my parents' house without a chance to talk to Rosy about the average guy.

Yesterday when I came back from my parents' Rosy was all dressed up and had organized everything in her apartment as if she was waiting for a special guest for a celebration. She looked very happy; I hadn't seen her that happy ever since I started seeing the simple man. She told me that she had decided to marry the average guy and he was coming to see her. Then she started talking about him without a pause. I could clearly see that she was in love with the average guy. I couldn't be any happier for her.

Rosy's brothers were not very happy about Rosy's decision to marry the average guy because they wanted her to marry someone whose family was politically connected. For centuries, marriages have been used to strengthen one's influence in the society.

When two people get married, it not only bonds the two people, but also forms a new relationship between the two families. The bride's and the groom's family adopt each other as their own. By marrying an average guy, Rosy had ripped her brothers of that opportunity. But they were happy to have her married than stay unmarried.

Rosy and her future husband have decided to get married in two weeks. I did think that was too quick but looking in Rosy's eyes, I can guarantee that those two weeks are going to be like two decades for her. She is eager to spread her wings and fly away with the stranger she met two weeks ago.

The average guy is not a stranger to her anymore; she has met him several times in last two weeks. I also met him a few times and I am more and more impressed with him every time I meet him. He is wise, thoughtful, and mature. I think he will make a very good husband for Rosy.

THE FLATTERER

"So, how have you been?" the oncologist asked me as he dried his hands with a paper towel, directing me towards the examination table.

I saw my reflection in the window as I moved away from it. Suddenly I became self-conscious about my looks. I always take care of myself. I spent half an hour in front of the dresser before going to my appointment in the morning; there was no reason for me to feel unconfident about my looks at the moment.

But I was meeting the simple man after thirty long years; it was natural for me to feel a little nervous about my looks.

I had to remind myself to focus on my disease not on my looks because I was certainly not there on a date.

"Pretty well except this cancer I got." I replied with a smile.

"You look great." He said.

"What a flatterer" I thought to myself.

I remember how he used to flatter those middle aged women back in the days by complimenting their look. His theory was that flattering is healthy for both the flatterer and the one being flattered. People like compliments, he used to say, more specifically women like compliments about their appearance. It makes them feel good about themselves, and there is nothing wrong with making someone happy.

"The fancy word for this is diplomacy." And then he would wink at me. That used to be his response if I complained about him complimenting everyone. I guess some habits are hard to change, especially if they yield the desired results.

"Are you still with me?" he frowned at me.

I realized that I had been staring at his face the

entire time. I hadn't heard anything he said. It took a few minutes to switch my mind back to the reality again.

"Yes," I replied, "I guess I can't run away from you, can I?"

He looked a little puzzled.

"I mean, you are my doctor." I clarified.

I am still not sure if he knew who I am. The history and physical exam session was very standard; he remained ultra-professional the entire time. He did not ask me anything beyond what a doctor would ask his patient. I was feeling a little different when I felt his hands on my body during the physical examination. I had not thought I would experience his touch again. I almost wanted to forget that I was a cancer patient on the examination table.

Frank Sinatra's song "Fly me to the moon" was playing in my mind.........

WEDNESDAY, JULY 30TH

When Rosy came from work today she burst into the room in excitement and told me that she had submitted her resignation. She was so happy that she was almost jumping up and down. She will move to another city with her husband after she gets married. I am happy for her but I feel sad for myself.

I am so used to having Rosy by my side. Whenever I needed a partner for anything, I could completely trust Rosy to support me. At times we both might have taken each other for granted, but we never were too tired, too sick, or too busy to turn our heads away from each other when one needed the other.

That had changed for Rosy after I met the simple

man. I have not been able to spend as much time with Rosy as I used to, and that made her feel lonely and abandoned. Rosy has a clingy, dependent personality. Once she trusts someone, she clings to the person like a leach. She is very demanding of the relationship but she is also equally generous in giving her best to it. I know she will make a great spouse to the average guy. She has been a completely new person in last two weeks. I am thankful that Rosy has found love.

Love is an amazing thing; it has the power to change the world. The simple man says love is nothing but dependency. But I think love is that feeling that gives you hope when you are feeling most hopeless, it is that feeling that inspires you to live when you think there is nothing to live for, it is that feeling that makes you smile when you are feeling blue, it is that feeling that encourages you to spread your wings and fly when you feel disabled, it is that feeling that emancipates you when you are trapped.

SUNDAY, AUGUST 17TH

Rosy got married yesterday. She was glowing in that bridal outfit. She was the happiest I have ever seen. I had thought I will be happy to see her married but deep inside I was feeling different. I was feeling lonely; I was feeling as if part of my heart was being ripped permanently.

I knew Rosy will no longer be around to share every funny, sad, or serious little thing that happened every day. She will no longer be there to stand by me and support every stupid opinion I had about whatever in the world.

Rosy is no longer my partner in crime. I can no longer make shopping plans, dinner plans, and movie plans, and inform her at the last minute. From now on, if I want to see her or even talk to her I will have to think about the convenience of her husband and her new family.

Rosy is not just my best friend, she is someone's wife now. The simple man says everything in life is temporary; friends, relatives, wealth, fame, success, they all become history one day. One can find happiness by learning to let go! What choices do we really have?

THE TRUTH

Reality struck when the oncologist started talking about the disease and all the treatment options. He repeatedly reminded me to take a deep breath and calm down as I continued to interrupt him with questions.

"So how long do I have?" I interrupted him again.

"Well, I don't know." He replied. That was not what I wanted to hear.

He continued, "We will need some more tests to determine our best options. At this point, all I can tell you is that your cancer is very aggressive."

"In other words, you are telling me that I am

dying?" My voice was breaking as I spoke.

"We all are. Do you know anybody who is not dying? Any one of us in this room could be dead tomorrow. Just because you have a cancer and I don't doesn't mean you will die and I will not. Life is unpredictable."

We had had that conversation before; the talks about life, the transient nature of life, and the unpredictability of death. I have witnessed the transient nature of life more often than most people. Why, at this stage of life, did I need him to remind me that life is transient?

May be I needed to hear it from the same magical voice, with the same wisdom and calmness that drew me closer to him many decades ago. My mind kept switching between the past and present.

"One option would be to enroll in the clinical trial." He sounded a little optimistic when he talked about this clinical trial.

He told me that the clinical trial regimen has been effective in other types of cancers, and it is the regimen with fewer side effects. However, they are not certain how well the regimen will work in this type of aggressive cancer that I have.

I am not a big fan of uncertainty but what better choice do I have? Even if the regimen did not work on me, I will still feel good knowing that I was able to help expand the science of medicine. Hopefully the information I will contribute will help other cancer patients in the future.

Couple of deep breaths was all it took for me to decide on my treatment options. I did not want to wait; I did not know how long I had to live but whatever time I had, I wanted to live productively. I was relieved to know that the treatment modalities in the clinical trials were relatively less toxic to other organs.

"I am an organ donor; I don't want those toxins to damage my healthy organs. I want them to be of use to someone when I die." I told him as I communicated my decision to enroll in the clinical trial.

"You have a big heart." He complemented me for being an organ donor, and he left the room.

"Too big that it is holding you inside it for all these years," I thought to myself.

We parted with the plan to see each other again in three days after my labs were in. When I asked for another appointment in three days, the nurse was surprised that he wanted to see me so soon.

MONDAY, FEBRUARY 28TH

Rosy's husband called to tell me that Rosy was in the hospital with severe bleeding. He sounded very nervous. Rosy had called me just a month ago to tell me that she was pregnant. I remember how happy she was to find out that she was pregnant. Sony thought that Rosy's decision to get pregnant six months after marriage was too soon but I am in no position to judge that.

The decision about when it is appropriate for them to start a family is something only Rosy and her husband can make. I think it is an honor for any woman to be the mother to the children of the man she loves so deeply. I too hope that the simple man will honor me some day by allowing me to be the mother of his children.

Rosy's husband told me that she had an ectopic pregnancy that led to a ruptured fallopian tube, and there was no way of saving the pregnancy. I can't even imagine what Rosy might be going through right now. I can only imagine how devastating it can be for the mother to lose her unborn baby.

Rosy and her husband were very excited about the prospect of having a baby; they had already thought about names, and started to look at the designs for the baby's nursery. Besides the trauma of pregnancy loss, the possibility of not being able to conceive again can easily throw Rosy into depression.

I am very scared for Rosy, thinking about all the possibilities of bad outcomes. Having worked in the medical field, I know the limitations of medical science. I know some women who had ruptured fallopian tubes; I have cared for many in the hospital.

Rosy needed a surgery to remove the ruptured tube and to stop the bleeding. I just wish I could hold her hands when she came out of the operation room. I just wish there was some magical way for me to be there with her. I feel so helpless and guilty that I cannot be there for

Rosy when she needs me the most.

I can't stop worrying about Rosy. The simple man says he would write a prescription for worry pill if worrying made anything better. I know that worrying about things beyond my control is not going to do any good.

Who has the power to change what the omniscient, omnipresent, omnipotent almighty has sent her to the world for? But when my best friend is going through the hardest time in her life, I can't sit here and not worry. I could not even talk to her when I called in the morning; she was all knocked out with drugs.

TUESDAY, NOVEMBER 21

Things have changed so much in my life since I wrote in this diary last. Some good things have happened, some sad things have happened. There was a lot that could have been written, but I had no courage to write that Rosy actually died. I didn't want to believe it, but the truth is truth whether I believe it or not.

I lost my best friend on the same day I got my dream job. I guess life is a mix of happy and sad moments. There were many questions surrounding Rosy's death. Why did she die? Could she have been saved? Who is at fault? and so on. I too wondered if she would have been alive today had she not wanted to be pregnant again. Only the omniscient creator of ours knows the answers to all of our ifs, and buts.

Rosy's death has challenged the human inside me who at times forgets how insignificant it is in front of the almighty. Despite having everything I wanted in life, I feel empty right now. Just when I thought I was done with sad news, mom told me that the lady whose son I was helping to go to school had decided to send the boy to an orphanage.

That is the six- year old boy I met last year when I went to drop my niece off at the local private school. The boy was cleaning the messy toilet at the school when I saw him that day. I couldn't stand the sight so I asked the principle what was going on.

The mother of this little boy had been trading his labor for his education. The boy's father had gone missing for years; the illiterate, unskilled mother did not have a job. The mother wanted to send her son to be a servant to some family in the city but he was still too young for that position. She wanted her son to go to English school but could not afford the tuition.

The boy cleaned the floors, cleaned the toilets, and even wiped the school children if they had accidents. He also brought water and tea to the teachers when they wanted it, and transferred files and books from rooms to rooms as needed. He came early to the school so that he could get the rooms ready for the day, and stayed late to finish up cleaning and organizing. The mother could not afford the school uniform, so the boy wore old, ripped, faded uniforms given to him by other students.

When I told what I saw in the school to my family and friends, everybody acted as if nothing was wrong with that. Child labor is part of the wealthy's culture here. Most of the privileged kids I went to school with or I now work with have grown up knowing and accepting the fact that having a child servant is the way of life.

Whether they are doctors, engineers, entrepreneurs, politicians, social workers or teachers, anybody who can afford to feed one extra person aspires to employ a child servant. I will have to think very hard to find even one well off family that does not employ a minor as a servant.

Even though the government schools don't charge tuition, many poor parents can't afford to send their children to school because they need their labor to support the family. They have to make choice between staying hungry and getting education. Sending their children to be servant to wealthier people means the children are less likely to sleep hungry, have opportunity to get education and build connections.

Not every poor parent who wants to send her children to be servant at a well-connected, wealthy family is able to do so because there are more poor than riches. There is competition everywhere, and the riches are skeptical about the child's loyalty and ability to keep up with the work demand while attending school. The masters prefer boys over girls because boys are physically stronger, and when they become teenagers, there is less risk of them running away with someone or getting pregnant. But girls are also hired if the master's family knows the girls' family or if the girl was recommended by someone they know.

Servants are not employees. The servants are on duty at all times, are not paid by hours, are not entitled to sick leave or any kind of leave, and do not need appreciation or respect for what they do. Servants live and eat at their master's house, wear the used clothes given by their masters, and are more loyal to the master than employees would be.

In other words, servants are like family members with no rights and privileges a family member enjoys. The opportunity to build this kind of close relationship with a well-connected family is no less of an honor for the servant's family.

In addition, the political and business connection of his master helps the child servant get some kind of employment in a government office or similar institutions when he grows up. In case of girls, the same connections help the girl servant find a husband with stable job. It sounds horrible to think that everything the riches in this country enjoy, wear, eat is soaked in children's sweat. Nevertheless, when I turn my head and see the hungry child dying from famine on the streets, I don't know which one is worse.

THE LOVE

I have barely started receiving the treatment for my caner, I already feel defeated by it. I looked in the mirror and almost did not recognize myself. I looked miserable. Baldness is not the only thing the cancer treatment has given me. My mouth is too sore to eat or drink anything. I am so tired that getting a cup of water from the sink feels like a chore. I have not written in this diary for so long because I have no energy for that either. My hands and feet are burning with the neuropathy the drugs have caused. I can't sleep in the night because my body hurts from being in the bed all the time.

On the bright side, this illness has given me another opportunity to realize how blessed I am. My daughters are by my side almost all the time. I have received overwhelming support from my friends and well-wishers. People have offered to bring meals, take me to doctors' appointments, help me with household chores and all sorts of things.

I really love the natural human instinct to make a difference in others' lives. Like the simple man used to say, "life is beautiful because of the beautiful people that surround us." And more than anything, I got to meet my love again because of this illness. What more can I ask for?

I do not want my daughters to ruin their careers for me. I asked them to go back to their normal routines, but how can a person have a normal life when her mother is fighting cancer? I may be the one with cancer but my illness has affected not only me but also my family and close friends. They have made adjustments to to their normal life to accommodate my cancer.

I never thought having one disease can change your life and the life of people around you so much. What the family members who take care of their loved ones with terminal cancers, dementia, and other end stage diseases go through is beyond words.

I joked with my daughters that they are lucky that I am dying of cancer, and will not live long enough to have dementia and forget who they were. They didn't think the joke was funny. I told them sometimes we need to laugh at ourselves.

It is not easy for children to see their parents suffer and go from an independent healthy person to the one who needs assistance with everything from using the toilet to changing her clothes. But Saipal says those of us who are able to spend the last few days of their loved ones' lives together are blessed.

Kris Allen's song "Live like we are dying tomorrow" keeps playing in my mind............

FRIDAY, DECEMBER 3ʳᴰ

After discussing what I saw that day at the school with the simple man I realized that the world needs more help than I can offer. But the scene of the child sweeping the school floor kept waking me up from my sleep. I decided to help the lady with the boy's education so that he won't have to clean the school's floor in exchange for his education.

The boy was doing really well in his class. I had offered to help as long as they needed help but the mother could not trust me as a permanent solution because I was unmarried and she was afraid that once I get married, my husband may not allow me to support them anymore.

121

The mother believed sending him to the orphanage would ensure that he will have food to eat, will get treatment when sick, will have clothes to wear, and will get education. But the orphanages do not accept children whose mothers are still alive. To convince the orphanage that the boy did not have a mother, she had to legally severe all her ties with him. That could also mean that she will no longer be able to see him. But the mother had made a decision to trade that relationship for what she believed was her son's better future.

My heart aches to know that the mother had to make such a tough choice. I feel like crying today. I wish I could talk to Rosy but she is dead. Life has to go on no matter what happens in the world. Adaptation is the only answer to the quest for harmony in life. Rosy was another example of a woman who made tough choice for the sake of motherhood.

Rosy was crazy about having her own baby; after her first ectopic pregnancy she decided to get pregnant again; she knew the risk, there was a possibility of another ectopic pregnancy and the rupture of her only other tube. There are many women who have had successful pregnancies after a rupture. Neither Rosy and her husband nor I expected that her desire to be a mother could be fatal. Rosy's husband and I tried to convince her to adopt a child rather than risking another pregnancy. But Rosy had made up her mind.

Rosy survived another ectopic pregnancy, ruptured tube, life-threatening internal bleeding, and another abdominal surgery. But she could not survive the aftermath of the incident. When she found out that she had lost both of her tubes, she lost control of her mind. Rosy went into severe depression. And one night Rosy went to sleep and never woke up.

Despite being so common, mental illness is often under diagnosed and under treated in our society. I will never know if Rosy got the medical attention she needed because I did not even know she was severely depressed until the night before she died. I had been talking to her husband about her and he never told me that Rosy was depressed. I wonder if there was something I missed.

I know it is not Rosy's fault to want to have her own child. The society looks down upon women who can't bear children. Rosy is easily affected by others' opinion of her. Even though she trusted her husband, she was insecure about her relationship. She was afraid that her husband might leave her for another woman if she could not give him children.

I want to cry my lungs out. Rosy is gone from this world, the simple man is going halfway across the globe next month, I will be lonely after the simple man goes to America. Even though Rosy was far, there was comfort in knowing that she was there when I needed someone to listen to me without opinion, and without prejudice.

The simple man is different. I can discuss with him about everything in the world but emotion is one topic I can't discuss with him because there is no common ground. He is ultra-pragmatic; he thinks separation and death are part of life, and says that we need to accept them as such. But just because they are part of life does not mean that they are easy to deal with. Sometimes I don't know if being practical is supposed to be living with no emotions.

THE BIG PICTURE

The diagnosis of cancer is frightening because it is possible that the cancer will kill me. But I am not the only one who is dying. Everyone that I have ever known, ever seen, and ever met, every one that has ever been born has died or will die. Rosy died, Renu died, my grandfather died, and so did hundreds of millions of people that came to this world. What big of a deal is it going to be if I die too? I stopped worrying long time ago. When you stop worrying, you feel liberated; your mind can think clearly and can see the positive side of everything.

Like the simple man said, I don't know of a one person who is immortal. What difference will it make if I die today, tomorrow or ten years later? In the big picture, the number of years doesn't matter; in fact, nothing matters in the big picture. Name, fame, wealth, power, they are all trivial in front of death.

It doesn't matter if you are the wealthiest person in the world, it doesn't matter if you are the most powerful person in the world, it doesn't matter if you are the most beautiful person in the world, you will have to die one day. What will you do with your name, fame, power, and wealth after your death? Ten years after your death, only a handful of people will remember you.

Hundreds of people die in this world every second, many of them from conditions other than cancer; many of them from conditions that are preventable. It does not matter whether I die from heart attack, stroke, cancer, or a car accident; death is what it is, unpredictable, unavoidable, undeniable.

What enables us humans to deal with this cruel fact of life is love; the love for self, and for another human. Love gives hope, and faith makes love and hope possible. To me, faith is not about saying a prayer or following certain principals defined for us by others. Faith is my ability to connect to the higher being whenever and wherever I wanted to. Faith is knowing that the almighty will guide me when I am lost.

When my daughters were small they used to ask me what the biggest thing in the world was. One night they argued if the biggest thing in the universe was the earth or the Sun.

When I told them that the Sun is bigger than the earth and that there are more than one hundred billion Suns, many of them bigger than our Sun, my older daughter Saipal said, "will I look like a dust if you look at me from far away in the sky?"

The eight-years old girl was very disappointed when I told her that our earth will probably look like one of those sand grains we see in the beaches. And suddenly I realized how insignificant we humans were in the big picture.

After that night, every time there was a conflict, an unpleasant situation, or something that hurt their feelings, I reminded the girls to look at the big picture, to think about the Universe, and understand how trivial everything else was. This approach helped us keep everything in perspective while dealing with the adversities we encountered from time to time.

We did not buy new clothes every season; we did not buy every new gadget that was out there. Some people asked me why I always wore the same shoes. I reminded them that there were hungry children who needed food more desperately than I needed a new pair of shoes; there were sick children who needed treatment more than my girls needed their birthday parties.

My daughters knew that before they painted their toes, before they bought a new garment, before they asked for a birthday present, they needed to set aside a portion of their income or allowance for those children who needed food, who needed mosquito nets, who needed medicine for worm infestation, and those who needed school supplies.

I still remember their faces glowing with a sense of accomplishment every time they saw the pictures of the children they had helped. It was not too long before they started asking for opportunity to help the needy child. Good deed is contagious; soon many of their friends joined them in helping the less fortunate. It only takes one person to change the society.

SATURDAY, MARCH 19TH

I called the simple man on his mobile when I arrived at the bus stop but his phone was switched off. It was already five O'clock; he should have been done with the clinic already. I thought may be some sick patients took longer than expected. I waited in the bus stop for an hour but he did not come. It was raining heavily. The streets were flooded. It was getting darker.

The crowd started to gradually ease off at the bus stop but there was no sign of him coming. There was no telephone booth nearby; the rain was pouring so heavily that I would have to be soaked in water to go out to make a call.

I waited for another hour; there were only a

handful of people waiting for the last bus of the day. All the shops around the bus stop were closing. I rushed out of the bus stop waiting area when I saw the telephone booth closing. The fellow allowed me to make one call before he closed the store. The simple man's mobile was still switched off. This is the same place we had planned to meet. I came exactly on time. I don't know why he didn't come. The last bus was already there and filling quickly. I hopped in.

This is not the first time I have waited for him for two hours. But every time I waited for him, he always came, even if it was for a short time. And he was almost always prompt in answering the phone. He never left me in darkness like he did last night. I couldn't sleep last night thinking about all the bad things that could have happened to the simple man.

Among several things I learned from the simple man is positivism. But ever since Rosy died, negative thinking keeps crippling me before I can see the positive side in anything. I feel like everyone I love will die in front of my eyes and I will not be able to do anything.

I kept asking myself why he did not come to see

me last night even after making the plan. Why was his phone switched off? He has been talking about this other girl quite often these days. It is possible that he was with her. But why would he make plans with me if he was going with her?

He is honest; if there was anything like that he would have told me. He is reasonable; he will not do anything like this for no good reason. The weather was bad last night, driving is crazy in this town; I kept worrying about him all night.

I prayed for the simple man's safety. May be the mobile towers were damaged by the heavy rain and his phone wasn't working. May be his bike had problems and he couldn't get it fixed. There are so many things that could have prevented him from coming to see me. I argued with myself about all the possibilities.

Sometimes I want to buy a mobile phone just to hear the simple man's voice whenever I want to. But the mobiles are out of my budget and I won't really have any use of a mobile phone after the simple man leaves for America next week.

I want to spend as much time with him as I can

when he is here. I don't know if we will meet again after he goes to the USA. My parents and relatives are putting pressure on me to get married. I get calls about marriage proposals almost every week. I don't know how long I can continue to ignore their nonstop nagging. I don't know what the future will bring. The thought of marrying someone else other than the simple man gives me goose bump.

I really hoped that I could meet him for lunch. But he was telling me about all the people that he needed to meet, all the paperwork that he needed to complete, and all the other things that he needed to get done before he left. I was not sure if he would have time for me. I don't know why, these days it seems like I come at the bottom of his priority list. But I guess I need to understand that he is getting ready to move to the other side of the planet, it must be more work than I see.

The nearby telephone booth does not open until after noon on Saturdays; the telephone booths just outside the hospital are open twenty four hours. Part of me said I should probably go out to call him. But the other part of me was not prepared to handle a broken heart again in case he was busy.

I feel very emotional these days; every little thing makes me want to cry. I didn't want to spend my day off crying, in case the simple man didn't have time for me. Fortunately the rain had stopped, and the sky was looking clear. I headed to the telephone booth the moment the clock hit twelve.

In less than a week he will be on the other side of the world; a place so far away that when it is day here, it will be night there. He says it is the place that stands for freedom and justice. The place that he thinks will offer better opportunities for him.

But it is a foreign land, they speak different language, they eat different food, they celebrate different festivals, they wear different clothes, and they think differently. I don't know how his life will be like in such a place. It gives my bones chills when I think about him going so far away.

Just as I had hoped, the simple man was fine. He wanted to meet me right away. I was thrilled. I didn't ask him what happened last night, I didn't need to know. I wasn't even mad at him for not showing up. He told me that he called me at my work in morning, and was waiting for my call all morning long. What a fool I was to waste my morning in doubt not calling him. I can't wait to see him again. God knows how much I love this man.

THE IMAGINARY FATHER

I was miserable from the side effects of the treatment until yesterday but I am already feeling much better today because I have an appointment with the oncologist. I must have over done the makeup and hair in excitement because Uma offered to redo it. Uma, my youngest daughter, was two days old when I first met her. I used to fix her hair and dress every morning to get her ready for school and outings. Now that little girl has grown up into a smart young woman, and is getting me ready for an outing. She is soon going to be a gynecologist. Time flew faster than I had anticipated.

My other daughter Saipal is putting together the list of medications and questions for the doctor, and getting all other items ready for my appointment. Both of the girls will go with me to my appointments today. They are thrilled to finally meet the man their mother so deeply loved and enthusiastically talked about for as long as they can remember.

The simple man was like their imaginary father; after all, his name is there in their birth certificates. This morning we are preparing for my doctor's appointment but it feels as if we are getting ready for a thanksgiving dinner, an eagerly awaited family reunion.

The simple man has not given me any indications to believe that he knows that I am the same girl who he had proposed to some thirty years ago. But there is something about his aggressive approach in curing my cancer. I don't know if he is equally aggressive about curing other patients too or he is more interested in curing me because he still loves me and he wants to save me at any cost.

But that might just be a wishful thinking. He is very pragmatic; he believes in solving the problem and moving on. He has his own personal life. Why would he be any more interested in curing me than curing his other patients? He is just doing what a compassionate doctor would do.

Donna Lewis' song "I Love You Always Forever" keeps playing in my mind ....

THURSDAY, MARCH 20TH

I was lying in the bed with the simple man thinking how wonderful it would be if I had the power to freeze the time. I wouldn't ask for anything more if I could feel this way forever, if I could keep looking at his powerful eyes for the rest of my life, if I could rest my head on his shoulders and find my world in him forever. How beautiful would it be if I could spend every evening of my life in his company like this? I wanted to preserve those moments forever. So I asked the simple man if I could take his pillow and the bed sheet with me. I wanted to feel his smell when he was gone. He laughed. I was about to cry, and then he said something else.

He told me that he was with another girl last night

138

when I was waiting for him at the bus stop in that pouring rain. He said the girl took him (I don't know if he took her or she took him) to Tango, the most expensive restaurant in town. He has never taken me to Tango, but he spent the evening with another girl in that restaurant. I was heartbroken, I was feeling robbed, I wanted to cry but I could not decide if it was even worth my tears. He knew that I loved him, I had nothing to say. I moved his hands away from my shoulders and closed my eyes.

He has many female friends, some of whom he gives more importance than I feel comfortable with. I do not want him to think that I am jealous; therefore, I try to act normal in these kinds of situations. I know that there is nobody else who can take my place in his heart, but I still feel insecure when I see him with other girls. I feel like I am being weighed against others; but each time he tries that, I come out heavier. I reminded myself that our relationship was based on trust and one night of poor planning should not be allowed to shatter it.

But I needed to let him know what he did last night was not acceptable to me.

"If you had plans with someone else, you should

have told me, I did not have to wait for you in that rain." I said after a while without looking at him.

He knew he had broken my heart, and he was prepared to deal with it. He put his hands back around my shoulders and pulled my chin towards him.

"I didn't have any plan with someone else but this girl was very insistent." He replied in a soft voice.

I was not sure if he wanted me to believe that he was a victim of some sort or that was his way of apologizing. His response made me angry.

I almost wanted to scream; "now you want me to believe it is all her fault? She might have told you to turn your phone off too."

I looked at him, his eyes were telling me he was really sorry; but he didn't apologize. He is very stubborn about not verbalizing his feelings. I can't even stay angry with him; he melts my heart with his honesty.

I took a deep breath and replied calmly, "it would have been really nice if the phone was not turned off, I would not have worried so much about you."

He gently rubbed my back and said, "yes, I should

have kept my phone on."

For some reason I could not get the anger about last night's incident out of my head. I was trying to enjoy his company but was feeling stifled. The simple man's hand around my shoulder wasn't really helping calm the emotional hurricane inside me. Part of me wanted to forgive him but the other part was looking for opportunity to retaliate.

I was looking for opportunity to hurt the simple man's feelings just the way he had hurt mine. I knew just how to do that. I got up from the bed and told the simple man that I needed to leave because my aunts had brought a marriage proposal for me and I was going to meet the guy for dinner.

It was true that my aunts had brought a marriage proposal for me. But I had already turned the proposal down with some made up excuses. So there was no meeting planned with any guy. Why waste my time and his time if I already know of my decision? But I was dying for revenge, so I lied to him about the meeting and dinner.

The simple man knows I am under constant pressure from my family to get married. My family will not let me get away with those excuses anymore because I have already finished college.

He pulled me closer to him and said, "let's get married. You don't have to deal with that anymore."

At first I couldn't believe what I heard. I wasn't sure if he just got carried away by the situation or he really wanted to get married. I looked into his eyes, they were full of love.

I knew he was determined. I felt numb, I lost control of my emotions, and I did not know if I should cry or if I should laugh. I hugged him tight. We soaked ourselves in the moment.

THE PLEASURE THEORY

My interactions with the simple man are rather formal; strictly about my disease and treatment. Unlike my appointments with my PCP and other providers with whom the conversations are also about kids and family and things outside of my health, appointments with the simple man are all business. I never asked the simple man about himself, or his family. What will I do by knowing? His personal life is not my business. In my last appointment, the simple man said that he read my book '*pleasure theory*'; how did he even know that the book existed?

Did he read the book just because he knew that I wrote the book? And how can he say with certainty that the book was written by me? I haven't told him or anyone else in the clinic that I have authored books. Does he know more about me than I think he does? He had asked me about my family, my social history, work, and everything else during my first visit. That was part of the health history; apparently everything in your life has something to do with your health. But I did not mention the books to him because I don't believe they have anything to do with my cancer.

My name is very common; the author could have been someone else with the same name. And when did he start reading those kinds of books? He had told me decades ago that he used to be voracious reader during his high school years. He said he had read biographies, books on world history, civil rights, science, fiction and everything else. And anyone who has conversed with him can tell that he is a well-read person.

But the simple man I knew did not read anything other than news, medical books, and journals. He occasionally asked me to summarize the bestselling books I had read. I am not a New York Times bestselling author; I do have a good number of regular readers but it is difficult for me to imagine that the simple man would be one of them.

He is a busy doctor, he is involved in many other philanthropic causes and medical researches, he may not have time and interest in reading a book about happiness from an ordinary author like me. But he says he did, and I know the simple man does not lie.

Did he resume reading books after moving to the US? Everybody reads books here; when I first came to this country, I was amazed to see almost everyone in the New York City subway holding a book in their hands. That was a cultural shock for me, someone who came from a country where illiterates outnumbered those with the ability to read and write.

I haven't been to NYC in a long time, it might have changed now. That was a time when there were no smart phones, tablets or e-readers. Now it seems impossible to imagine our lives without these gadgets.

I know that the simple man embraces technology happily. It is possible that he developed the interest in reading books after the books went digital. Or is he married to someone who loves to read and he also got a hang of it? Did he ask his wife or someone else to summarize the book for him? But again, he recited few sentences from the book as if he had read it multiple times.

But why would he read my book "pleasure theory" when there are many other bestselling books in the market? This is very unusual of him. Does it mean that he thinks about me outside of the clinic too? I wonder if he sees me in his dreams.

I had not seen the simple man in my dreams for years, and now I see him again almost every day. People say dreams are the product of the subconscious. These days my dreams are very complex, many times they don't make any sense to me. Last night I had a dream where I was with the simple man aboard a driverless bus.

Driverless vehicles are nothing new these days but it was not a self-driving vehicle with a human behind the wheels. The bus was driving itself, there was no visible driver; I had faith that the bus knew where, when, and how it was supposed to reach its destination, but I was afraid that other people on the road may stop the bus if they saw the bus without a driver, and they may punish the passengers of the bus for riding a bus with no visible driver. The simple man did not seem to be bothered by any of that, he was enjoying the ride.

THURSDAY, MARCH 24TH

Rosy and I had visited a very popular fortune teller right before Rosy's marriage. The lady analyzed the various grooves and lines in one's palms to predict one's future; and I had heard that her predictions were very accurate. I didn't really believe in that kind of stuff but Rosy insisted me to have my palm read too, so I had my palm read as well.

I got really interested because she could accurately predict so many things about my life that she had no way of knowing. She read palms of about 20 people every day, there was no way she could research each person's past or present. There had to be some truth to whatever she was saying about their future.

What she said about my future didn't really bother me at that time but it is keeping me awake right now. Thinking back, I remember that the fortune teller told Rosy that she had a short life, and that Rosy will never be a mother; that was one of the reasons Rosy was obsessed about getting pregnant. The lady also correctly described the physical characteristics, the nature of the job, and the geographic location about Rosy's future husband. But the fortune teller was wrong about a few other things.

After the fortune teller predicted Rosy's marriage, I also asked her if she could predict mine. To my surprise, she told me that I was deeply in love with a man who also loved me equally. She gave the simple man's descriptions as if he was standing in front of her, and she was looking right at him.

But she warned me that if I married him, I will be the cause of his destruction. What a curse; the timing of my birth was such that marrying the love of my life can be equivalent to pushing him into a hungry tiger's cage.

The simple man's sudden marriage proposal has thrown me over the moon but my heart is divided.

The part of my heart that does not want to believe

in the superstitions says, "this is the man I love so deeply and want to spend my entire life with, I should not end this relationship based on some palm reader's prediction."

But the other part of my heart that also loves this simple man so deeply says, "what if her predictions are true? Would you rather stay apart and let him flourish or marry him and destroy him?"

For eternity, I was waiting for that moment; my ears were yearning to hear those words from the love of my life. But when the moment finally came, I am feeling totally torn. I can give up everything in this world to be with my simple man, but I can't allow myself to be the cause of his destruction.

I don't know if the fortune teller was right about this one, but I can't afford to experiment it. If I truly love my simple man, I must part ways with him. After all, I am a Manglik, a person born during the time when the planet Mars is in certain position in the solar system.

While there is no scientific evidence to prove the widely held belief that Mangliks have strong negative influence on their spouses if they married non-Mangliks, I also think that there had to be plenty of anecdotal evidences about the negative effect of the Manglik marriages to convince people from all walks of life, including those who are educated, to believe in it.

One of my cousins, a Manglik too, was married to a non-Manglik man and he later fell from the roof and is paralyzed from shoulder below. I have heard plenty of other incidents for which a Manglik spouse is blamed.

Since this is a belief specific to people from this part of the world, there is no research that I am aware of that focuses on the outcomes of marriages between Manglik and non-Manglik individuals. Even if the belief was unfounded, not many people have the courage to take the chance and test, validate, or refute it. People say that there are different ways you can avoid the negative effects of the Manglik, one of them is to marry another Manglik, in which case, the negative consequences of one cancels the other's negative consequences. The simple man is not a Manglik, so this is not an option for us.

There are other astrological remedies that are believed to remove the bad effects of a single-Manglik marriages. My cousin went through a ritual in which she was first married to a banana tree or something like that, and then married to her husband. The ritual was supposed to cancel the negative influence of her being a Manglik. But it apparently did not, and she was blamed for her non-Manglik husband's accident and subsequent paralysis.

I don't know if my cousin's husband's accident was the result of her being a Manglik or not, but I won't be able to live with myself if I marry the simple man and something bad happens to him. I have to go away from him.

How can I communicate this to the simple man and make him understand the reasons behind my decision? The simple man does not believe in this kind of superstition. I also did not believe in baseless superstitions but this one is different. Just because there is not enough information or scientific evidence about something does not mean that it is not true. I can neither prove nor dispute the belief. And I don't want to experiment it for the sake of proving or disproving it because the stakes are very high. I can live without the simple man but I can't let my selfish desire to be with him ruin his life, in case the beliefs were true.

I used to think that I could not live without the

simple man. But my heart said something different to me today. The same heart that loves him so deeply told me that we were not made for each other. Love is not dependency, it knows when to let go. Love does not end when the loved ones depart. Love does not hold one back, it enables one to move on.

Very soon these days of shared laughter, these never ending talks about life, death, and happiness, the lectures about discipline and dedication, the jokes about unmade beds and lost underwear will end. So will the dream to be each other's partner in helping the less fortunate of the world.

There is no better time than this to end my relationship with the simple man. He is leaving next week, I think it will be easier for me because I will not be able to see him or talk to him even if I had the temptation to do so. Phone calls are not going to be easy either because of timing and how expensive it is to call internationally. And, the simple man would not be able to easily get a hold of me on the phone because I don't have a mobile phone and he will have to call me at work.

But the simple man will not agree with it if I told

him about my plans now. He knows I am a Manglik, but he believes that if the almighty has brought you so close to someone that brings happiness in your life, the person already has enough positives to cancel the negative consequences of the cosmic influencers. He also told me about one of his family members who was also a Manglik and has been happily married to a non-Manglik for many years. Regardless of what he says and what he believes in, I am too afraid to take the chance. There has to be a reason why god sent me to the earth as a Manglik.

THE DILEMMA

What an exhausting day. The doctor ordered more blood tests, scans, and more investigations. I was ready to go to bed by the time I came back from my appointment on Tuesday. I used to run marathons, I don't know if it is my age or it is the cancer that is eating my body, I can't even go to the bathroom without having to pause to catch a breathe. The other day I was feeling a lot better so I went cycling without realizing how cancer had taken over everything about my life. I could barely go a mile and that was it. I spent the rest of the day in the bed.

I told the doctor that my symptoms hadn't improved with the treatment. In fact they were only getting worse, and I had those horrible side effects. The doctor said he also thought the cancer wasn't responding to treatment but needed more tests to decide the next course of action. I am not sure if my body is ready for another round of tests and experiments but my daughters think I should try. The doctor told me that he is retired and he will transfer my care to another doctor. I will have a different doctor when I go for my next appointment.

I also found out that I was the only patient the simple man was actively managing. All of the other patients had already been assigned to other doctors. He had retired the same week I first saw him, but he continued to see me. Everybody in the clinic treats me like I am some sort of celebrity, no wonder. I was the reason the retired doctor was leaving all his other philanthropic work behind and staying there. I felt embarrassed, they probably knew more about me than the information they officially collected.

And just as I thought, the simple man knew more information about my disease than he shared with me in my last visit. He knew I didn't have any treatment options left, he knew the test results were likely to show that my cancer had spread all over my body but he waited until the results came to share this information with me. He calls it optimism; he said there was a thin chance that the cancer could be treatable. He "did not want to leave any stone unturned." He wanted to unlock every possible exit before telling me that all the doors were closed. But the wish of the omnipotent, omniscient, omnipresent cannot be altered; I have only a few weeks left on this earth, in this body.

I asked the simple man if he approaches every patient with this aggression. He told me that he knew I had a very slim chance of cure but he wanted to do everything possible. He apologized for putting me through the treatment and side effects.

He said, "It is very difficult when you find out your loved one is dying, you want to do everything that is out there. Your only goal becomes saving their lives even if it means putting them through horrible side effects and poor quality of life."

My daughters shared his view and wanted me to go through every procedure that had even a slim chance to save me. This dilemma is common among the families of terminally ill patients. I often hear patients and family members say, "I want everything done to keep me alive." Some people believe not doing everything could mean giving up. I am an optimist, and I do believe that one should not give up as long as there is reasonable evidence that the chosen option has a potential to achieve the desired goal. The reasonableness and the desired goal may vary from one person to another.

To me, the quality of my life is more important than the number of days I am kept alive. Will I opt to live last few weeks of my life dealing with horrible side effects, doctor visits, and ambulance rides because the medicine has a potential to prolong my life by two months or has a five percent chance of curing the cancer? Perhaps not. I would rather live those days comfortably surrounded by the people I love the most, and doing things that are most important to me. Treatment of cancer is expensive; even if I didn't have to pay the full cost, it has to come from somewhere. Why not let that money be used for saving someone else's life than prolonging my life by two months? The simple man agreed with me.

I asked the simple man why he took the "do

everything that is out there" approach in treating me.

He said, "I knew in my heart that we will meet again someday, but I never thought that we will meet like this. I wanted you to live so that we could start everything all over again."

I felt an urge to cry, not because I was told that my days on this earth had come to an end but because I had put the simple man through the grief again. I had done a grave injustice to him by first mysteriously disappearing from his life and then coming into his life like this and dying on him. The simple man did not tell men what he did when he found out that I had decided to go away from him, but he wanted me to tell him everything that happened after he left.

THE TOUGH DECISION

My decision to separate from the simple man may sound sudden and haphazard but it was one of the most thought out and well planned decisions I had made in my life. It was also the most difficult decision that I had to make so far. He was the center of my life at that time; and that was the most important reason I decided to separate from him.

I was not superstitious, but I was also not courageous enough to challenge the astrological beliefs people in that part of the world had held for centuries. Future is unknown, and when I had the opportunity to avoid the potential mishaps of the future, I decided to take it.

I will never know how much truth was there in the fortune teller's prediction about me having negative affect on the simple man if I was married to him because I did not experiment it. But I also did not regret leaving the simple man then, and I don't regret it now.

The last day I saw him was the day I helped him pack the suitcases. I had written a letter to him explaining my decision but I could not decide how and when I would give that letter to him. I inserted the letter in one of his important files that he was going to open when he reached the USA. Before I left his apartment that night, I told him that I had written him a letter that I wanted him to open only after he was comfortably settled in the new place. He agreed.

After the simple man left for the US, I started to feel very strange. Everywhere I went, I missed the simple man; there was not one street, one square, one park and one open sky that did not remind me of him. I did not need to forget him but I needed to have a normal life without him. I was not lonely, I had many good friends who would do anything for me; but I felt a vacuum inside me, there was something missing from life. I realized that if I wished to fill that vacuum in my life, I needed to go away from the town, and everything that reminded me of my life with the simple man.

I don't know when he read the letter, what he thought, and how he reacted after reading my letter because I had cut all my connections with him. One thing I was confident about is that he knew I was like a river, flowing in one direction and there was no going back. He knew me well, he was aware that even if he tried, his efforts to change my decision were likely to be futile.

He had tried to contact me through a friend, probably after he read my letter; but I did not want any contact with him because his voice had that magic that had potential to shake my determination. I cried all night, asking the almighty why I had to make such a tough choice. The almighty said to me that we don't always get everything we want, there is more pleasure in giving than getting. This was one of them I needed to cherish.

I packed my bags and boarded a long-distance bus without knowing where I was going and for how long. I arrived at a beautiful city by the rolling foothills of mountains. I decided to make it my home, finding a job at a local hospital was easier than I had imagined. This town gave me the shelter I needed from my past.

I am cancer, by nature I prefer to hide inside my shell when I am not comfortable with the outside world. I fell in love with my new life in new town with new friends. But the vacuum inside me was still there, I needed to make a difference in others' lives, I needed to help the less fortunate make a better life for themselves.

THE LOWER CASTE WOMAN

The mother of one of the pediatric patients in the ICU reminded me so much of Rosy. She was tall, fair skinned, had large, beautiful eyes, and long, dark hair, just like Rosy's. She was by her daughter's side all the time, rubbing her unconscious daughter's feet and kissing her forehead. She looked very tired, and extremely sad. She looked pregnant, and it looked like she had not eaten anything in days. I had not seen any other person other than the mother who visited the patient. So I asked her if she would like to join me at the cafeteria for lunch.

Her name was Renu. She was eight - months pregnant and had not eaten a meal for two days. Renu was not educated but she was very wise. Her parents died in a mudslide when she was young, she grew up working for a master for whom generations of her family had worked as servants. Renu never went to school, but learned to read and write when a local nonprofit offered a night literacy classes for girls and women like her who could not go to school.

Renu said her master started to sexually abuse her when she was still very young, and she got pregnant when she was sixteen. But the master denied fathering the child and threatened to kill her if she told anybody about it. He gave her some money and asked her to abort the baby. But the abortion was unsuccessful. Then the master coerced one of his other servants to admit that he fathered Renu's child and forced the two to get married.

Renu described her husband as a very nice man who loved her daughter like his own. But he wasn't happy with the master's abusive treatment of the poor, and joined the local insurgents in hopes of finding a better life for his family and other poor people like him. One night her husband left with a group of armed insurgents, to fight for the poor, and disfranchised people's rights. She never heard back from him after that. People said he was killed by the government forces during an armed attack, but neither his name was in the list of the dead insurgents nor did she receive any compensation from the party. She was pregnant with her second child at the time.

But the misfortune did not stop there; her two-year old daughter suddenly got sick and was brought to the ICU. Renu blamed herself for her daughter's illness because she thought the abortion pills she had taken when she was pregnant with her might have caused the little girl to fall sick.

Poor Renu did not know that her daughter had Japanese encephalitis, a disease transmitted by mosquitoes, and not something caused by the abortion pills. Her daughter died the next day. Renu cried when she found out that she lost her child to a mosquito bite because she could not afford a mosquito net. I could not hold my tears when I felt the mother's helplessness.

Renu was optimistic that her daughter would survive because her daughter was under the care of highly qualified doctors in a highly regarded hospital. I could not tell her that we were doing our best to save her daughter's life because that would have been a lie. Her daughter died not because her disease was incurable, but because Renu lacked voice, she lacked money, she lacked power, and those people upon whom she had put her faith lacked compassion.

Renu gave her daughter ambu -bag breathing for two days in the hallway of the pediatric unit before she was transferred to the ICU. Since the hospital has only one critical care unit for both adult and pediatric patients, ICU bed availability can really be a challenge, especially when some politicians decide to take some rest and come to the hospital.

Renu's daughter did not receive the much needed ICU care until later because the ICU bed was being occupied by a well-connected patient who was kept in the ICU after a minor outpatient procedure after which most people go home.

Summer is mosquito born disease season in the southern part of the country. Mosquitoes are there pretty much all year long but they kill thousands of people every year during the summer. The beds and hallways of the pediatric and adult medical wards are full of meningitis and encephalitis patients during that time.

There is always scarcity of skilled manpower to

provide any type of skilled patient care. Patients depend on their relatives for all care except injectable medications. Sometimes, the family members also change the intravenous saline. It is not unusual for the family members to ambu-bag a patient until the ICU bed and ventilator becomes available.

Renu was devastated by the death of her daughter. Knowing the situation she was in, I could not allow myself to leave Renu with the only option to go back to her abusive master. I told Renu she could stay with me until she could find a job and a safe place for herself. Renu had been through a lot during her two decades on this earth but nothing was as difficult for Renu as was losing her child. Optimism was her strength, and both Renu and I knew time was the only answer. She had to live for her unborn child. Renu felt the need to be strong, to overcome that emptiness, and the feeling of not having a purpose in life.

Sometimes I think tiredness, pain, discomfort, and all these feelings are luxury. When you do not have a choice to rest or relax, you have no luxury to feel tired or feel the aches and pains. You keep going. That is exactly what Renu did; her pregnant body desperately needed rest but she picked up some cleaning and dish washing jobs immediately. She pretended to be ok, perhaps her body's need to rest was not as strong as her mind's need to forget the loss that she had been through.

My family, close friends and relatives weren't happy to know that I had allowed Renu to live with me. Renu was from a lower caste, the untouchable. She was not supposed to be anywhere close to the upper caste people. My mother was worried that allowing Renu to live with me could ruin my chances of finding a good husband.

People thought I was very naive in that I had taken the burden of keeping a heavily pregnant woman at my house. Renu was anything but a burden to me, she was a hard-working, intelligent, young woman who needed a little help to stand on her own feet. She was very mature for her age, and her heart was as beautiful as her face. I knew Renu would soon find her independence and happiness.

Renu gave birth to a healthy, beautiful girl. She named her Saipal, the name of a himalayan peak in the northwestern Nepal. Renu hoped that her daughter would be as strong as those himalayas that stood tall and poised regardless of the weather. Saipal had brought so much joy in Renu's life, she was happier than ever. Renu had started to work at a local soap factory. There, Renu found her soul mate, and she married him soon after.

Not long after they got married, Renu's husband decided to join thousands of fellow countrymen in one of the gulf countries for employment. I could see the mixed emotions on Renu's face on the day her husband left. There was the pain of separation but there was also joy in the hopes of better future.

Upon reaching his destination, Renu's husband found out that he was deceived by the manpower agency that sent him. He was paid half of what was promised, and had to work longer hours in harsh working conditions. But the only option he had was to work hard so that his family would have a better life.

Renu was optimistic that things would get better with her husband's job. Then suddenly she got a phone call saying that her husband was critically injured in a work related accident. He died the same night. Her dreams, hopes, happiness, and optimism vanished in the horizon just like the sun vanishes in the night. But Renu's sun was not coming back in the morning, it was laying listless inside the coffin, and there was darkness everywhere.

The optimistic, happy, positive Renu had died with her husband's death. She had exhausted all her reserve of prayers, perseverance, endurance and patience. One night Renu left Saipal with me saying that she had decided to go on a pilgrimage to bury her husband's ashes in the holy Ganges. She never came back.

I became Saipal's mother. I was unmarried, in my late twenties, and raising a child that was from a low caste. I was under pressure to get married but my mother was extremely worried that no decent man will marry an older woman like me who was raising a low caste child.

My friends and family told me to get married and have my own child if I was so eager to be a mother. I was also advised to hand Saipal over to an orphanage. I did not give birth to Saipal but she was still my daughter, I could not let her be orphan as long as I was alive.

You don't have to give birth to a child to give it the mother's love. I remained firm in my decison to keep Saipal and my mother remained firm in her decision to get me married. At that time, her only purpose in life was to see me married.

To keep my mother and other "well-wishers" happy, I met with a few so called smartest bachelors they had chosen for me. Some of those men belonged to the social elite circle who, having connections with the influential politicians and bureaucrats, promised me promotions and big raise if I married them. Some lived overseas and promised me better future if I married them. Others were self-proclaimed geniuses who thought they were doing a big favor to me by meeting me there.

None gave me a good reason to marry them. Each seemed to agree that they were not really seeking a life partner, but instead a permanent servant who was educated yet docile, who did not need be paid, and who contributed financially. Not even one man agreed to accept Saipal in his life.

I chose Saipal over each one of them; but the pressure to get married kept getting intense, and Saipal continued to face discrimination everywhere. Her being from a lower caste was enough for many people to refrain their children from playing with her. I had no choice but to leave the town without letting anyone know where I was going.

Saipal and I started a new life in a new town. The town gave us anonymity for some time but it did not protect us from suspicious eyes. To make our lives simple, I had told everyone that I was Saipal's biological mother. People were very interested in knowing about our personal lives, most importantly, knowing why I was a single mother. When I went to register Saipal in the childcare center, the application form required father's name.

Who else could I think of to be my child's father if not the simple man? I knew the simple man would have loved to have Saipal as our daughter.

THE ARRIVAL OF UMA

I started working in the maternal ICU after moving
to the new town. I used be saddened by the sight of many
young women dying from complications of pregnancy and
childbirth. Many of them were seeking medical help for
the first time during the entire pregnancy. With no proper
antenatal care and safe delivery options, if survived, many
of them ended up with long term or permanent
complications from childbirth. Then the husband would
marry another woman.

I was very touched by the situation of a nineteen
year old patient who was admitted with severe eclampsia
and went into cardiac arrest after her c-section. This

patient was brought to the hospital by her husband from a remote village. She never had antenatal checkups because there was no healthcare facility nearby and they did not have money to travel. The patient was on a ventilator, unconscious. Their baby girl was born prematurely and needed to be observed in the neonatal until for a few days.

The husband could only speak his local language, and was having hard time communicating with the healthcare team. I grew up in a town where the local language was very similar to what the patient's husband spoke. Though not fluent in his language, I was able to communicate with him and serve as an interpreter for the team. With no money, no knowledge of the culture, language, and the medical system, the husband was very anxious and frightened about the entire situation.

The patient's husband was very nervous that his wife was going to die and he would be left with a needy newborn girl to take care of. The husband worked as a construction laborer, carrying bricks and sandbags at building sites. He said he had no money and no help to take care of his daughter if his wife died. The patient's husband abandoned her and the newborn girl when the patient's health deteriorated. The mother died, and the newborn girl had nowhere to go.

Girl children are not favored in some families, particularly because of the hefty dowry the parents need to pay when the girls get married. Some people go to the extent of emotionally torturing or physically harming the woman if her parents did not give enough dowry or if she gave birth to a girl child.

It is ironic that in the society where female deities are worshipped as a symbol of wisdom, power, and wealth, the female members of the society face some of the worst treatments one can imagine.

The hospital authorities were trying to contact a local orphanage to hand the baby over because nobody came forward to claim relationship or to take custody of her for more than a week after the father left. I wanted to adopt the baby girl but the hospital authorities were against it because I did not have a husband, and they would not allow a single woman to adopt a child. I tried to convince them that I was an experienced mother but my request was denied citing the adoption laws that required the husband (adopting father) to sign the adoption papers.

That incident raised further questions about my

mysterious single motherhood, and why I was interested in adopting the baby girl that was abandoned by her father. I was an outsider in the town with no family and relatives nearby. Some people suspected that I could be some sort of child trafficker who will eventually sell the baby to some foreign criminals or a group like that. Others took this as an opportunity to poke their nose into my personal life.

Incidentally, the orphanage was unable to accommodate the baby because the baby was born prematurely and there was a risk of disability in the baby due to a questionable hypoxia after birth. Since there were no other options available, the hospital authorities agreed to release the baby to me; I named the baby Uma, the hindu Goddess of power. But I could not legally adopt her until I produced a marriage certificate showing the name of the husband.

That was not the first time I had faced legal discrimination and social hurdles for being a woman. When I first applied for my passport at the age of twenty three, my application was rejected because my father was not physically present to sign the authorization documents for my passport application. The laws required a male guardian, the father, the husband or another male relative to be present in front of the passport officer to sign the passport application for any woman under the age of 35 applying for a passport.

I knew that I would never be able to adopt my daughters legally if I did not do something about it. And even if I adopted them legally, they would never be able to get a citizenship until they got married because women in this country can get a citizenship only through their father or their husband.

The official birth certificates in this country do not include the mother's name, but have to have the father's and the father's father's (paternal grandfather's) names. It does not matter who the mother is, she is just an insignificant woman who gave birth to the man's child. But the laws in this country can be flexible if you let your wallet do the talking. I borrowed the simple man's name in place of my daughters' father.

My daughters got their birth certificates but I knew that the hurdles would not stop there for me and my two daughters. In every step of their lives Saipal and Uma would be scrutinized about their roots, their family, and their identities. One needs certain degree of autonomy to do what one is good at doing.

As long as I was being punished for being a woman, I could not do what I was good at doing. Therefore, I decided to move my family to a place where my daughters would not face discrimination for being women, for being born to a lower caste mother, and for labels that were assigned to them from birth over which they had no control.

My life after I moved to the USA is documented in my purple diary.

The simple man held my hand the entire time he read my diary. He read each word as if he had an exam on it. Few drops of tear rolled down my cheeks as he kissed my eyes one last time before I let go of his hand and my heart beat for the last time.

AFTERWORDS

Cancer sucks, death sucks even more. But we humans don't have the power to stop either of them from messing with our lives. They enter our lives whenever and wherever they choose to. Cancer is so common that each one of us have known someone who has dealt with the disease; some of us have lost a loved one to cancer. Common does not always mean simple, and it also does not mean we know everything about it. The diagnosis of cancer, regardless of the disease's curability, is almost always nerve-wracking, even for healthcare providers like the main character of this book who is a veteran nurse.

The primary male character's personality traits and the quotes are inspired by my husband Binay, who, in his own words, "deals with death every twenty minutes." When Binay decided to become a cancer specialist, many of his doctor friends said that he was going into a depressive specialty because the majority of cancer patients die. Binay, with his signature optimism, always replied, "there are only two kinds of diseases that can be cured with medicine; caners and infectious diseases." Many people, including healthcare workers, are still unaware that many cancers are curable, and there is hope for cancer patients.

But Cancer is not the only reason I wrote this book. At a personal level, my husband Binay and I have been touched by death very closely. In June 2008, we lost Binay's mother to a fatal stroke. The day she had stroke, she had just finished packing for her trip to the USA to meet her first grandchild that Binay and I were expecting at the end of October. Four months later on October 25th, 2008, I woke up to a fetus that had stopped moving. We rushed to the hospital only to be told that our daughter had died inside me. It was two days before my due date. My pregnancy to that day had been uneventful.

Those two incidents changed our lives forever. The sudden death of my perfectly healthy mother-in-law at the age of fifty, and the sudden and tragic end of my healthy pregnancy reminded us once again that life is as unpredictable as it can be, and we must to do more for the mankind. Binay and I both have had the privilege of working with individuals and family members who deal with chronic and terminal illnesses. Each day we are reminded to live life one day at a time, to help the less fortunate around us, and to never forget that there is always a morning after a night.

When I suddenly lost my daughter to stillbirth, I thought of those mothers, wives, daughters, fiancés, girlfriends, sisters, and friends who wave good buys to their loved ones in the military before they are deployed to a foreign land, and the loved ones never make it back home. Their suffering is not smaller than mine, and there are thousands of people like me who have lost their loved ones to sudden, unexpected circumstances. What helps them get through is their faith and love. If you have been touched by death, you know what I am talking about.

As a nurse, I had the privilege to work with critically ill people of all ages, seniors with dementia, individuals with chronic kidney diseases, and folks with disabilities that interfered with their activities of daily living. It does not matter who you are and what you have done in your life, when you are dealing with such life threatening illnesses, your life revolves around it. It was humbling to see how a small act of kindness would put smiles on the faces of people who were suffering. You don't always have to know them, but you can still make a difference.

I will be donating all of the proceeds from the sale of this book to Binaytara Foundation's (BTF) cancer projects. I invite you to visit the BTF website at www.binayfoundaiton.org and join us in our endeavors to make a difference in the lives of less fortunate around the world.

Proof

Made in the USA
Charleston, SC
25 November 2014